HUGE STEPS

A TWIN MFM MENAGE STEPBROTHER ROMANCE

STEPHANIE BROTHER

ISBN: 9781976991318

CONTENTS

PROLOGUE
ABIGAIL

Up until now, I've only seen them in photographs.

Jared and Jamie.

All it takes is the thought of their names for a flush to rise up my neck and color my cheeks.

I know I need to stop this but I can't help it. You know that feeling you get sometimes when you see a guy. That primal feeling that tells you that you're supposed to mate with him and make babies, regardless of the fact that you've never even uttered a word in his direction. That's how I feel about Jared and Jamie. It's as though there is something in my physical make up that knows them and craves them, despite the fact that they are, for all intents and purposes, strangers.

Strangers who are going to be my stepbrothers in a few months.

I'm too young to be thinking about making babies. Sweet sixteen and never been kissed, but I guess all that means is that I'm pumped full of hormones and urges that have never had an outlet.

Dad and I are on our way to the barbecue restaurant across town so that the formal introductions can be made. I've met Dad's girlfriend, Natalie, before but they've kept us kids apart up until now. Dad's finally proposed so I guess that means everything is going to become permanent and it's worth getting the families together.

I wonder how Jared and Jamie are feeling about getting a new stepsister. I wonder what they thought of the photograph they've seen of me. Probably nothing like the things I've been thinking about them. With their perfect smiles and gorgeous eyes, they could get any girl they wanted. My thicker than ideal thighs don't seem to be having that effect on the boys at school.

I wring my hands, fussing with a sharp bit of nail that I wish I had a file to deal with. I gaze out of the window, not really taking anything in but hoping for a distraction. I shouldn't be this nervous but I can't help it.

"They're really nice boys," Dad says as though he can read my mind or feel my angst.

"I'm sure they are."

"You're gonna get on like a house on fire," Dad adds cheerfully. "You always used to say that you wanted a big brother to take care of you."

"That was when Jonas was picking on me and I wanted a big brother to beat the crap out of him."

Dad chuckles and pats my knee. "That boy liked you…he was just trying to get your attention."

"That boy should have been taught that liking someone doesn't excuse abusing them."

My dad is quiet for a while and I regret letting so much sharpness into my tone. "I wished you had a big brother then too," he says softly and shrugs. "Now you're gonna have two."

"I'm sure they're not gonna be interested in protecting me from the douchebags in this world. They don't even know me."

"It's not going to take long for us all to get better acquainted. And they are good boys. I know they'll be stepping into the big brother role in no time."

I know Dad's just trying to be nice and reassuring but his continuous mentions of Jared and Jamie becoming my brothers is make me feel a little queasy. I've imaged then in just their boxers with their muscular chests and washboard abs. I've imagined them kissing me one after another until my mind has melted into a puddle of goo and my legs can no longer hold me. I've imagined naughtier things that I would never admit to another human being. Things that are definitely not sisterly, that's for sure. Things that fill my mind as we pull into the parking lot.

Natalie's car is already there and dad pulls in next to it. He's all smiles as we follow the waitress to the back of the restaurant. My stepmom-to-be sees us first and she's up and out of her seat as though we are arriving dignitaries rather than a middle-aged insurance salesman and a slightly disheveled teenager who has no idea how to make the best of herself. Even from behind, the sight of Jared and Jamie is overwhelming. When they turn I'm almost knocked off my feet with lust.

Damn.

I know I'm going to humiliate myself. I know I'm not going to be able to act normally. They're probably going to go home and laugh about the pathetic girl they are going to be stuck living with.

3

Except that isn't what happens at all.

They might be gorgeous but they are good boys too. That first night in their company, I come to realize something. My new stepbrothers might just be the most perfect men in the world, but now they're completely off limits because we're going to be related.

The thought makes me almost lose my mind.

1

ABIGAIL

It took me three days to finally decide on this dress.

This is what I'm thinking as I hear the whispering outside. Whispering that sends a rush of embarrassment through me. Embarrassment and panic are a terrible combination.

Three. Days.

I kept going back and forth between this one and the softer, lighter-colored dress that was more my style. Still, the saleslady was pretty adamant about the dark satin texture, and I guess I thought that Cody would like this one best. I was in such a blur of planning and dreaming that my feet were hardly on the floor, and my head was barely screwed on tight enough.

At least the dark color of the dress does a good job of hiding the tear stains on my lap...

Outside there's more whispering, the snippets I catch echoing softly around the ladies' restroom. The way they're trying to keep their voices down is almost laughable. Numbly wiping at my wet cheeks, I sniffle and clear my throat, feeling ridiculous. Dramatics have never really been my thing, and I hate the idea of being the object of anyone's pity.

The phone vibrates in my hand, startling me, and my heart sinks just as it starts to pathetically float upward in my chest. It's just my friend, Bailey. Judging by all the exclamation marks blurring together on the small watery-looking screen, I'd say she's just a tad concerned.

But it's not him, so I set the phone back down for a moment, not bothering to really read the text. I worry at the corner of my lip before quickly tapping the keyboard and redialing, hoping for the hundredth time that he picks up.

Maybe it's traffic.

Maybe he had a flat tire.

Or maybe he was just, well, nervous. This thought fills me with another rush of panic.

The engagement party was set to start at six o'clock on the dot, and I know he didn't just suddenly forget the time. Not with the way his mother mentioned it every other sentence lately. Besides, Cody is just way too efficient at life, and usually way too honorable with his social etiquette for something like that to be the case. He's either lying in a ditch on the side of the road somewhere or ignoring me—there is no in between.

A loud, quick knock breaks me from my hazy thoughts and I immediately smooth down the front of my dress as if whoever is on the other side of the door can actually see me. "Yes?"

"Abi, please come out," my father's strong but subtle voice pleads.

But if I come out then it means it's real. That whatever is keeping my fiancé from showing up to our engagement party is real, and no matter what it is, it's not good. No news is good news in this scenario.

"I'm just..." but I let my voice trail off and shake my head at myself. There's really no point spending the next however long until I hear from Cody, sitting on this grimy toilet. With every bit of effort that I can muster, I stand up and smooth down the dress again, suddenly feeling very stifled by it.

It takes a moment to wash my face enough to get the messy lines of makeup off, but I emerge from the ladies' restroom looking as put-together as I possibly can, considering.

Dad sighs, wrapping one arm around me. "We don't know what's keeping him, Abi. It could be nothing more than car trouble." My dad is known as a realist, and the doubt in his voice isn't exactly helping matters any.

I nod, not really wanting to agree with him since he and I both know how Cody's phone is practically grafted to his hand at all times, and if it were just car trouble keeping him back, it certainly wouldn't be impairing him from texting a simple 'I'm alive,' or 'sorry I'm late.' So, I let Dad guide me back into the elegantly-decorated room where everyone else is quietly mingling, doing their very best to avoid eye contact with me. My cheeks burn with shame.

"I'm going to check in with Natalie. See if she needs help in the back." Dad gives me a quick kiss on the forehead, squeezing me around the shoulders before heading toward the kitchen area of the banquet room. As much as I hate the idea of dealing with this dread in front of him, it would've been nice not to have to stand here alone, as if I'm some middle-schooler waiting on someone to shyly come up to me at a school dance.

Just as I'm about to find the seat furthest away from everyone else, a quiet sound catches my attention. "Abi!" someone hisses.

I turn around to see my best friend, Shay, leaning around the corner of the nearby exit, and I hop up. "What are you doing? I thought you were tracking down Mich…"

Cody's best friend, Michael, peeks around the corner too, as I rush over, the look on his face enough to stop me dead in my tracks.

"I found him," Shay says weakly, not even bothering to crack a smile like usual.

I do a quick survey of the room and as soon as I'm sure no one's paying me any attention, I slip outside to join them. "What's going on?"

Shay nods to Michael. "Tell her."

After shuffling his feet for a moment, he finally looks at me and shakes his head. "He's not coming, Abi."

It's like I hear the words nice and clear, but they don't mean anything in my head. "What do you mean he's not coming?"

"He called me about fifteen minutes ago while we were on our way to his place. He said there was no need to come…that he wasn't going to show up."

I'm aware of the stars coming out one by one overhead as if they're just poked holes through the warm, dark blanket of trust I've had with Cody for the past three years. "Was that all he said?" I ask, my voice gravelly. Shay reaches out to hold my hand, squeezing it.

"We showed up and uh, well…"

Shay's patience level immediately drops below zero as she huffs, "Jesus Christ, Michael, just fucking spit it out already! We got there and I made him tell us the truth. He said he didn't want a serious relationship right now and that it was a mistake to propose in the first place. He was also pretty wasted with a bottle of whiskey in his hand, so the rest of it was mostly just one long, unintelligible slur. It was like something out of some shitty rom-com Abi, I'm...I'm so sorry," she finishes all in one breath, pulling me into her arms.

I don't know how many times it takes me to catch my breath, but as soon as I manage to drag it back into my chest, it rushes out sort of like a slowly deflating balloon. "He...he..." But I can't finish the sentence because if I do then that would make it real, and things like this only happen in the previously mentioned crappy rom-coms.

This is real life.

This is my life.

"He didn't want to commit to you, he wasn't ready for any of it, and he was sorry, basically, is what I understood from it," Michael adds, looking as if he'd very much rather be anywhere else than in front of me and my splotchy face.

I step out of Shay's hug, trying to shake myself out of this weird daze, and think back on the signs. They were there, of course they were...his unstable moods whenever the engagement was brought up, his flakiness. Even before he proposed there were so many moments that I thought to myself that I was dealing with some kind of petulant child and not my boyfriend.

"This is my fault," I whisper, unable to help myself. I hold up my hand as Shay takes a step forward and shakes her head violently. "No, no, it is, Shay. I always made these lame excuses for him whenever he'd break his promises before, telling myself that he just had a lot on his mind, or that he had a terrible memory, or that I was just blowing things out of proportion. All the signs they were...they were already there. This was never going to work."

Shay's voice is lost in the fog of my brain as they both walk me back inside, and even though my parents and everyone else who has come up to me to tell me good-bye have been talking the whole time, I don't really listen. I know what she's saying—not to beat myself up about any of it, but it's kind of hard not to when I already had a feeling that something like this could happen with him.

This is what I get for falling for the class clown. Cody could never take himself seriously enough, not when it came time to get real about things. About our future together. I mean...even my own step-brothers who I've argued with plenty of times before, are more mature than Cody.

Someone shakes my shoulder, and I realize that I'm standing back inside and that the room has pretty much emptied out.

"Hey, honey. Why don't we go ahead and get you back home? The boys and I can make sure everything's wrapped up here," Natalie, my step-mom, whispers.

I nod. "Sure. Thanks, Nat."

She gives me a squeeze and behind her I see the twins, Jamie and Jared, sharing a dark expression. Say what you will about them, but at least they care enough to be angry at what's going on. While everyone else is trying to placate me, there's no doubt about how they feel. Not with Jared's stance solid and the veins in Jamie's thick biceps bulging as he balls his fists up at his sides. Unbelievable. My brain is misfiring so badly that my eyes linger on the two of them before I finally look away. Yes, because that's what I need right now—to be staring at them like a weirdo thinking things that I try to avoid because it's just not appropriate.

I watch the stars glittering above us on the way back to my dad's and Natalie's home. It doesn't take us long before we get there. I could probably make the case that I am okay to drive over to my apartment, but I tell everyone I need a shower and some major sleep instead. That way no one thinks twice about barging in on me in my old room, leaving me alone.

I'm able to put on a neutral expression for everyone else's benefit, but as soon as the door is shut behind me everything inside of me crumbles. I slide down along the door until I'm lurched forward, the sobs building up until they spill out.

I desperately reach for the stereo and put my loudest music on full-tilt, trying to drown out my humiliation and disappointment from everyone else's ears.

2

ABIGAIL

"Ugh," I groan, rolling away from the blinding light that's filtering in through the window by the bed. My head is pounding like I was run over by a truck last night, and I need some serious caffeine. Neither my dad or Nat drink coffee though, which means I have to put myself together enough to make my way back to my own apartment ASAP.

Before I reach the bottom of the steps, I can already smell the bacon and eggs wafting up from the kitchen. Sure enough, Nat is busy banging around, completely dressed and ready for the day, while I'm wearing an old tank top and a pair of worn jeans that couldn't possibly be any tighter around the middle—the only outfit I could manage to scrounge up in my old room. The elegant engagement dress has been tossed into the nearest corner until I can decide whether I want to set it on fire or not.

"Morning," I grumble, giving her a quick wave.

"Ah-ah-ah! Don't just take off without having some breakfast first!" she says, pointing to the place setting at the table that's already got a plate full of food and a whole glass of my favorite almond milk.

I look down at the food, my stomach betraying me by rumbling loudly enough for Nat to grin. "Well. Who am I to deny free food?" I say, slipping into the chair.

Nat tries to strike up a conversation with me—anything other than the topic of my pathetic sham of an engagement, that is—but I can't find it in me to reciprocate. I'm just not in the mood for talking, I guess.

Once I've finally scarfed down my breakfast, in more of a rush to get out of here than I should be, I push away from the table. "Thanks for breakfast, Nat."

"You don't have to thank me, honey. I just want to make sure you're okay, you know? I can't even imagine…" she seems to hold back though, deciding instead to smile and pat my hand from across the table. "Well, of course, you'll be okay."

The kitchen door opens and two tall figures pile inside, both standing behind their mother, leaning down to give her a kiss on the cheek. It's not unusual to see my twin step-brothers randomly popping over when there is food involved.

"Hey, Ma. We're sorry that we're eating and leaving, but we gotta get going," Jamie says, grabbing a few slices of bacon.

Nat looks at me, scraping the last bit of her food into her mouth before smiling up at her sons. "Hey boys, I don't suppose the two of you would mind giving Abi a ride over to her apartment, would you?"

Jamie shrugs, while Jared scoops up his own handful of food, nodding. "Yeah, that won't be a problem. Are you ready to go, Abi?" Jared has always been more deliberately thoughtful than Jamie, so this comes as no surprise.

He turns his gaze to me and it's so intense. I've never been able to work out if it's his general way of looking at people or if he just reserves the shiver-worthy bone-melting stares for me. Maybe I'm just so exhausted from everything that's gone on the past twenty-four hours that I'm just a bundle of frayed nerves at this point. "Yep. All finished," I say, pushing away from the table.

I thank Nat for the breakfast and throw my purse over my shoulder, following my step-brothers out the side door.

The trip across town is a quiet one because Jamie and Jared are too busy talking about their favorite football team to really notice me brooding in the backseat. It's probably a good thing. I'm mortified enough about yesterday without looking like I'm a complete wreck today. I can't wait to get to my apartment so that I can hide away from anyone watching me.

As we pull up to the curb outside my building, relief floods through me as I realize neither of them is making a move to get out with me. I mumble a goodbye and scramble to get out of the car, but before I can turn around and head up the steps, I hear Jamie knocking his wide fist against the window, He rolls it down, half leaning out of it. "Hey, Abi. We know you're going through some shitty stuff…if you need anything, you just gotta call, okay? We've got a couple places we have to be today but later if you want us to come and cheer you up."

My heart sinks. I know they're just trying to help, and as comforting as it is to know that the two of them are willing to hang out with me to make me feel better even while I'm a hot mess, I really don't think I'm up for it just yet. I swallow hard. "You guys really you don't have to…"

14

Jared leans over from the driver side, meeting my gaze. "We know that, Abi. But we don't want to leave you mopping…we're around if you need a distraction. And if we happen to see Cody on the street between now and then, well…"

"A few less-kindly words will probably fly, you can bet your ass on that," Jamie finishes for him, his eyes narrowing.

"Thank you," I manage to reply, not wanting my voice to sound as thick as it feels in my chest and throat. They've always been sweet to me but I've never had reason to see their protective sides. By the time they came into my lives as my big brothers, all the bullies had left me alone. Both Jamie and Jared's expressions soften.

"Seriously, Abi, just let us know if you need anything."

I take a step back away from the car and give them both a lame thumbs-up.

—

A hot soak in the tub doesn't seem to relieve me of the anxiety stirring around my brain, so I wrap my robe around myself and pad barefoot into the kitchen. I look at the champagne left over from the other night but as much as I'd welcome the cool trickle of numbness I know it could bring, I shared it with Cody.

So much has changed.

How can something that was once associated with happiness so quickly turn bitter?

There's a knock at the door, and a couple quick buzzes on the doorbell, letting me know who it is immediately. Shay.

"Oh girl, I should've known you'd be walking around in a daze. Look at you." She shakes her head, her dark curls bouncing as I let her inside the apartment and lock the door behind us.

I walk wearily back and take a seat on the couch. "I don't even know..."

She plops down the couch beside me, nodding. "I know, I know, honey." She pats my knee as though I'm a puppy who needs reassurance. "I just... I still can't believe he had the balls to just bail on you like that. I mean we all knew he was flaky as hell, but this just goes beyond everything else he's done."

"You thought he was flakey?" She never said anything like that about Cody before and Shay always says what she thinks. At least, I thought she did.

Shay rolls her eyes again. "He needed you to tie his shoes, girl. I know you might not want to hear this now, but you are so much better off without that douchebag."

My heart clenches. Part of me wants to hear her say terrible things about Cody so that I can believe that this situation I'm in is for the best. It's the part of me that's completely humiliated by what's happened. It's the part of me that wants to storm around to his place and hit him over the head with the champagne bottle from the kitchen and tell him exactly what a lowlife piece of shit he is. That isn't me though. I thought I knew Cody. I thought I was going to spend the rest of my life with him and I'm so confused about everything. All the plans that I had mapped out in my head have blown away like dust and I don't know what's going to happen now.

There are so many things I want to say...so much whirring around in my head but going over it all isn't going to make me feel better. I'm not the kind of person who shares problems. The shame of feeling more pity, even from my best friend, is definitely not what I need right now.

"I don't think I want to talk about it," I mumble, putting my head in my hand. Just keep my eyes open.

"Abi, you and I both know that you might as well get it out while it's still fresh. Rip off the Band-Aid. That way you can clean up, and move on with as little scarring as possible. I think you owe it to yourself to get over it as quickly as possible, don't you? Besides...isn't that what I'm here for, anyway?" she asks, nudging me. Shay's nurse anecdotes don't make it any easier of a pill to swallow.

"I guess. I don't know, Shay. I just don't understand how he could've done something like this. After everything I've put up with!"

"Well, you know what they all they say. Everything happens for a reason. You guys weren't meant to be, it's as simple as that, and I can't make any kind of excuse for his shitty behavior. I think you knew that trying to get a guy like Cody to commit to you wasn't exactly an easy task."

"You think I was too pushy?"

"Oh no, you don't, Abigail! You are not about to pull that crap with me, no way. You were way too good for him and everyone knows it. Including Cody"

I lift a shoulder meekly, feeling as though the words she is saying are true, but they still can't penetrate through the insane amount of guilt I'm starting to feel. "It's not even just about him being flaky though. It wasn't only about the commitment issues...he just didn't want me. He didn't think I was good enough for him."

Shay quickly stands up, half-dragging me up with her as she places a hand on my shoulder, keeping us both steady. "He knows that you are too good for him, and that's why he thought it was okay to ghost you like that. He thought 'well since everyone knows that I'm a piece of shit boyfriend to Abigail, why not live up to the title?' Plus, he probably couldn't commit to buying a brand-new pair of shoes without trying on every pair in the damn store. That's just the type of guy he is, Abi. You can't let yourself feel guilty about any of this."

I slowly slide back down onto the couch, my head feeling like it's stuffed with cotton, Shay's statements having a hard time making it through the muffled mess. Yeah, I definitely should've just closed the curtains and called it a night earlier when I had the chance.

"And before you tell me that you're going to need some time away from everyone to draw up into your little shell here," she says, gesturing to my apartment, "I got this for you." She hands me my paycheck from Dandies, the florist shop we both work in.

"I can't even take a couple days off tomorrow?"

The corner of her mouth quirks up but she shakes her head. "You need to come back to work, babe. You need to move on with your life, and the sooner the better. I know you. If I leave you to your own devices, you'll just lie around in your bed and go through about seven or eight different pints of Ben & Jerry's. At least if you go to work you'll be distracting. Plus, nothing says 'fuck him' quite like moving on and still getting paid," she adds, holding up her hands.

I sigh. "I guess, and I appreciate your concern for the wellbeing of my chunky thighs. I will go back to work... Soon."

That seems to satisfy her as she gives me a quick nod, but then her expression clouds over once again. "I'm not gonna be able to stay, babe. I promised my mom I'd pick up Jasmine from her ballet class today. But there's one more thing I wanted to chat with you about before I go."

She takes a deep breath and grabs my hand as if this information could change the world. And I thought I was being dramatic.

"Cody is an idiot, and I think we both know how terrible he is about making a rash decision and then immediately regretting it. He jumps into things without thinking, and he's flakier than my gramma's homemade biscuits. And he knows how to easily appeal to you, especially since you're so sweet and wear your heart on your sleeve. So when the jerk does start sniffing around again, trying to get back with you, just remember how much better your life will be without him in it. Okay? Can you just please promise me, Abi?"

The worst part is that I can't even get mad at her for saying this...she knows me better than anyone else, and she knows how bad I am at holding a grudge. It sucks, but I have to admit that she's right. "I promise," I whisper, shame blooming across my freckled cheeks.

Pulling me into a hug, Shay squeezes me and lets go, giving me one more smile. "Okay. I'll call you to check in with you tomorrow. And uh, I'll let Dandie know you'll be out tomorrow, too."

Once the door shuts behind my best friend, my shoulders sag. It was a nice little distraction to have her here with me, even though all we did was talk about Cody. But now that I'm alone in my apartment again, the same feelings creep back into my heart, and try as I might, not even my pint of Chunky Monkey can make me feel any better.

3

ABIGAIL

"Ouch," I hiss. I pull my thumb back and check out yet another fresh puncture from a rogue thorn. It seems that the single roses I'm working with are out to get me today.

"You all right? That's the third time today, girl!" Shay calls out from behind the front counter, thanking the customer as she hands her the bouquet of peonies she's just finished wrapping.

"No big deal. Guess I'm just not paying enough attention or something…"

I move on from the roses, having finished taking off the thorns, and look for the nearby ball of twine. The front doorbell chimes as Mrs. Riddle and her shorter, rounder friend Mrs. Johnson come in, cackling like a couple of old hens to each other. As soon as they see me towards the back, their expressions change immediately. It's like they've seen a ghost.

I can't help but watch them as they wander around the shop, no doubt waiting for Dandie to come out and have a quick bite to eat with them, gossiping about the town like they usually do. Except this time, I have a feeling I know exactly what they'll be talking about. Each time I catch them out of the corner of my eye, they're staring at me, whispering too low for me to hear. Even Shay narrows her eyes in their direction.

What started out as me being utterly heartbroken a few days ago has led to this crazy sort of rage building up inside of me. Everywhere I go I see people giving me these sad, pitying looks. I've even heard people talking about me and Cody, as if what happened between us as anyone else's business. And the more I see people whispering, gossiping about me, the angrier I get.

I grip down hard on the back of one of our chairs, trying to hold my tongue. By the time I realize the two older women are walking towards me it's too late to do anything but just stand here.

"Oh, Abigail. You poor thing, you. I'm so sorry to hear about… Well, what happened," Mrs. Riddle begins, reaching out to pat my white-knuckled hand. "I can even begin to imagine how you must be feeling right now."

"I'm quite all right, actually," I say through gritted teeth. "Just keeping busy at work."

Mrs. Johnson looks as if she is genuinely about to cry, and places her hand over her heart, slowly shaking her head. "Such a brave girl."

Are these two for real?

"Elizabeth! Patricia! I didn't realize you were already here," a familiar voice says from behind me. Dandie, our boss, twist her hair into a messy bun on top of her head, looking decades younger than her two friends, and forces a smile in my direction before touching my shoulder. "I hope you don't mind, hun, I have a new order that just got called in. Would you take a look at it while I'm out with the ladies?"

I know this is just Dandie trying to rescue me from her meddling friends, and I nod gratefully. "Of course, Dandie. I'll get right on it. It was nice seeing you," I say to both Mrs. Riddle and Mrs. Johnson, lying right through my teeth.

Waiting until the three of them leave the shop, I collapse against the chair, trying to calm down. How dare Cody put me through this...all this humiliation! I can guarantee that no one is busy bothering him with pitying looks. No, they save it all for me. I know they're thinking of me as just some pathetic girl who got stood up at the altar...and I never even made it that far!

No, what I really want to do is march my butt straight over to the Mayor's office, climb up on top of his desk and scream at the top of my lungs how much better off I'll be without his stupid son of my life. I want to tell him what a spineless moron he's raised.

I snatch the new floral order off the clipboard and take a look at it, sighing. It's an anniversary bouquet from Mr. Ventura, one of our favorite customers here. The man treats his wife like an absolute queen, so I don't find it surprising at all when I see the sheer size of the bouquet. Mr. Ventura would never stand up his wife in any way. Is it too much to ask for someone who would treat me the same way?

I'm busy in the back when I hear Shay calling for me up front. I peek my head around the corner to see both Jared and Jamie standing on the opposite side of the street outside the diner. I groan to myself as they look around before crossing over. The doorbell chimes and duck, not feeling ready to face yet more worried expressions and kind words.

"We know you're back there," one of them…probably Jamie, says loudly, eliciting a giggle from Shay, my obviously very traitorous best friend. "So you might as well come out."

I slowly make my way into view, getting hit with the full force of their presence. As hard as I try, I just can't stop the butterflies always form in my stomach when I see them. I can't stop the heat I feel in places that should currently be withering given my circumstances. I want to smile because, despite being identical even down to their birthmarks, they still manage to differentiate themselves so naturally. Jared's hair is messy and his shirt untucked. Jamie's hair is styled and his clothes are all neatly ironed. I love that I can tell them apart so easily. It makes that fact that I've always had a huge crush on both of them at the same time feel less weird. They might be twins, but they are obviously two very different people.

I already know that they're going to ask me to hang out with them at the diner for lunch and as much as I love the diner and know they'll manage to take my mind off my woes without even trying, I don't feel like leaving this store one little bit.

"It's lunchtime," Jamie says wiggling his eyebrows.

"I have this huge order in the back to do, guys. You go on without me."

"All work and no play makes Abi no fun," Jared says. He's got that bang on. Fun is about the last thing on my mind.

"I'm not really feeling all that hungry…"

"It's your lunchtime, girl," Shay says lightly, raising a brow at me. "You better get going before I have to tell Dandie that you're not eating now. You know how she feels about not taking breaks…" Total traitor. The twins grin and my shoulders slump. They're ganging up on me and it's so not fair.

"All right fine, fine, but I can't stay for too long. I really do have a huge order to get to back there."

Jared nods. "No problem. Shall we?"

As soon as we step into the diner my stomach rumbles, the sweet smell of rolls and coffee hitting me right in the face. I probably shouldn't mention that I went without breakfast this morning.

Sharon, our waitress, pops over with a none too subtle smile, practically drooling over Jamie and Jared as we settle into our booth. "Well hello there, fellas! Hi, Abigail! Do y'all need a minute to go over the menu or do you already know what you want?"

I push the plastic menu away from me, smiling up at her. "I'll just take a Caesar salad, Sharon, thanks. Oh, and a water with lemon, please?"

Jamie snorts. "What are you, a damn rabbit? Don't you usually get the All-Star burger?"

My mind immediately goes to the struggle I had trying to fit into my work pants this morning. I clear my throat. "No, it's fine. A salad is good."

"Really, Abi, we won't tell anyone. How about that burger?" The corner of Jared's smile quirks up and I can't help but look away. Food is not my friend.

"I'll take the chili dog with a side of fries, oh and an extra side of those crispy onion straws, and an order of wings to go with that. Oh… And yeah, I'll take a salad, too. With a Coke," Jamie tells Sharon, handing her the menu with an earsplitting grin. She looks as though she's about to keel over just by staring at them.

"O-okay," she stutters in response, looking absolutely dazed. "And you, Jamie?"

"Actually... I'm Jared," Jared replies sweetly. "I'd like to get the sampler platter, with the salad on the side. Both of us want thousand Island dressing, too, please."

All this talk of food is only making my stomach growl louder, and before Sharon turns away, I finally add, "I guess I will go ahead and have that All-Star burger, Sharon. Thanks."

As she walks away the twins start laughing at me until I join in, feeling silly.

"You don't need to worry about what you eat, Abi. You look good just how you are."

My cheeks start to flame again.

"And you've been through a lot of shit this week. You just need to relax, okay."

Jamie's words touch my heart and put a lump in my throat that feels like a bolder. I swallow and fuss with the cutlery in front of me, knowing that if I look up and see their gorgeous faces swamped with sympathy that I'll probably burst into tears.

I remember when our parents first got married, and Natalie and the two of them moved into our house. My mom had already been gone for close to ten years, so it had been a really long time since we had another woman around, and I wasn't sure of what to expect with Jamie and Jared, either. I had been so nervous, trying to be as polite and quiet as possible. They'd had to remind me that it was my home and that I need to relax then too. It's funny to think about that now, years later. "I guess," I mumble, unwrapping silverware from its napkin.

I assume they must be able to tell I'm close to tears because they immediately change the subject, filling the silence with stories from their morning. Jamie swears that he saw some kind of lizard in one of the toilets he cleared today and Jared reminds Jamie that they need to go and quote for a new job later on. It's the kind of conversation where I only need to listen which is good because I'm feeling too drained to engage much. I glance around the restaurant, hoping that my meal will come quickly and I can get back to work and bury myself in orders.

My stomach drops when I see a familiar face. Daniel, Cody's friend. We've never really gotten along, mainly because Cody told me about all the rotten things he did behind his girlfriend's back and, also because I got the feeling he resented the way that Cody spent so much time with me instead of his friends. Daniel doesn't notice me right away, and takes a seat at the counter, talking with one of the cooks.

Everything in me automatically tenses up when Sharon comes around the corner with a tray full of food for us, because Daniel's eyes casually follow her until they land on me. The hair on my arm stands on end when his expression darkens. I can already tell he plans on saying something before Sharon finishes doling out our plates, my stomach twisting up in knots.

Even Jared senses something's up, and he nudges me. "Everything okay?"

I wave him off, but when Sharon walks back behind the counter, I barely touch my food, anticipating it. I don't want to look his way again so I fix my eyes on the burger and take a deep breath, telling myself that I'm overreacting. He has no reason to say anything. Cody was the one in the wrong and I've kept my mouth shut since because causing a scene or spreading gossip just isn't my style.

"That Cody's friend," Jared asks. I look up at my stepbrother and nod. His face is stoical and his eyes watchful. "He's heading this way."

I can't help turning my head to look just as Daniel starts to slowly approach our table.

"Enjoying yourself?" His words are practically dripping with acid.

Both the twins turn to look at him, the tension between us all thick enough to cut. "Is there a problem, man?" Jared asks.

"Why don't you ask Abi?" Daniel says. "Going around town, making everyone feel sorry for you just so everyone turns against Cody. That's some amazing pity party you're throwing for yourself."

My cheeks are on fire as I meet his gaze and I'm about to say something in my defense when Jamie holds his hand up. "What the fuck are you talking about," he says, his voice menacingly quiet. "It's Cody who screwed Abi over."

I glance around the diner, feeling self-conscious as the heads of some of the other diners turn in our direction.

"You know he never wanted to marry you," Daniel says. My heart seems to stop from the humiliation. "You just kept going on and on about it and in the end he caved."

"You piece of shit," Jamie spits. I can feel his body getting ready to rise and I put my hand on his knee. Even as I'm trying to stop the situation escalating my mind is whirring. Is that really how it was? Did I hound Cody into proposing? My eyes well with humiliation. Is that what Cody is saying?

"Cody was lucky that Abi even considered saying yes and she's damn lucky that he proved himself unworthy," Jared says. "She's had a lucky escape."

Daniel laughs loudly and it's this that sets off the twins.

Both Jamie and Jared stand up, looking like a massive wall between me and Daniel. Without time to blink, Jared and Jamie haul Daniel up under his shoulders and easily take him outside, Jamie's mouth getting the better of him as he shouts loud enough for the whole town to hear. "You asshole! Get the fuck outta here. You ever come near Abi again talking this shit and you won't fucking be able to open your mouth again for a month."

I watch in horror, not because I'm not grateful that my stepbrothers are defending me, but because I know that this will only add to the gossip that I've been finding unbearable. I try to catch the sob that's threatening to rush out, shakily take a sip of my water, watching as my stepbrothers push Daniel out of the door and wait for him to take off, their arms crossed like two bodyguards. They wait another minute, talking to each other, before coming back inside, their expressions somber.

"Sorry about that, Abi," Jared says, shaking his head. "He had no right to say any of that. It's not like it was your fault."

"We should've just laid him out. Just one hit, that's all it would take, man," Jamie mumbles into his bite of food, still looking a little unhinged. "I dare the motherfucker to try that again."

Jared levels a look with his brother. "Let's just hope he doesn't. Abi doesn't need that kind of garbage in her life."

Jamie practically stabs at his food with his fork, his anger still very clearly on his mind, while Jared takes more careful bites, sizing everything up before looking over at me with a small smile on his face.

This is how they've always been...you could never miss how Jamie feels about any one given thing, while Jared keeps his cards closer to his chest. They may be identical, but they're like night and day in some ways.

"Thanks for lunch, guys," I say weakly as we head back into Dandies, the breeze sweeping my coppery hair all over the place.

Jared slings his arm around my shoulders. "You don't need to thank us, honey. You just concentrate on forgetting Cody and his idiot friends and getting that pretty smile back on your face."

Jamie tugs open the door to the shop.

Shay's standing behind the counter eyeing us all. "What the hell happened over there," she says. "I saw you guys hefting Daniel out the door."

"One of Cody's dickhead friends started mouthing off," Jamie admits, leaning against the front window. "And we handled it."

Shay studies Jamie and Jared for a minute, giving them a nod before turning back to me. "You don't look so good. Tell you what…I've already started on Mr. Ventura's bouquet, so why don't you take off for the rest of the day?"

The confrontation still has me shaken, and it takes me a moment to finally respond with, "I'm okay."

"You don't look okay, sweetie."

The twins look at me and nod. I guess I'm not that good at hiding how I'm feeling right now. As much as I hate skipping out like this on my best friend, I have to admit that getting out of here sounds better than staying. "Thanks, Shay."

"We can take you home. I'll take your car and you can ride with Jared back to your apartment," Jamie says, standing back up.

Instead of arguing with them over treating me as an adult and not some fragile doll, I sigh and thank them too. "I'm fine though," I add for good measure. "I'll...be okay."

4

JAMIE

"Son of a bitch. Did you eat the last of the pop-tarts?" I hold up the evidence—an empty box, half-filled with empty silver wrappers.

But Jared doesn't even bother to look up from his phone. "Hm?"

Bastard. He can pretend to be the health nut all he wants because we both know he has a not-so-secret stash of junk food hidden in his nightstand.

"I just picked this up the other night, too," I mutter more to myself since my brother is very obviously not listening. I toss the leftover cardboard into the recycling bin and start rummaging through the pantry, hoping to find something else for lunch. Usually, the two of us go grab it while we're out between jobs, but neither of us has had the chance to pick up groceries at the market this week.

"You know, since we need some food at the house, we should run by the store. And…I was thinking maybe we could stop over at Abi's place to try and cheer her up. She seemed pretty weirded out by that guy at the diner," Jared says.

It's funny how the so-called psychic twin connection can come into play sometimes. "Yeah, that's not a bad idea," I reply, scratching at the stubble I've been letting grow in for the past few days. "We could even pick her up a few things."

I try not to think about the spooked look on Abi's face, or even worse when her eyes were so puffy and red after Cody stood her up at their engagement party, because every time I do, I start seeing red. No one deserves to be treated like that. Especially Abi.

--

I knock loudly on the door, ringing the doorbell a couple of times just because, and stand back and wait. It isn't like we had to walk very far with the groceries anyway, not when Abi's apartment building is right next to our place. We didn't even plan on us living so close to each other, but I know it helps Sam, our step-dad, sleep better at night knowing that we're there if she needs us.

I hear her footsteps inside the apartment when she yanks open the door, and I'm surprised to see her already in her pajamas for the night. It's barely even past three o'clock. "What are you guys doing here?" she asks. Maybe we should have called first but at this time of the afternoon, it didn't even cross my mind.

Jared pulls out the bottle of her favorite red wine and the chocolate sampler box stashed inside, smiling at her. "Room service."

There's still a weird expression on her face, but she finally opens the door wider and lets us in. "Sorry," she mumbles softly, "My place is sort of a giant mess right now."

I wave her off because who am I to judge, really? My room looks like a fucking tornado hit it half the time. "You know we don't mind."

I don't know if maybe my words trigger something inside of her not, but in the same moment that I say them, her eyes immediately well up with big tears, her bottom lip quivering as she pulls her arms around her sides. I stare at my brother in alarm, not really sure what to do in an instance like this. I'm not exactly well versed with crying girls.

Jared clears his throat, taking a step closer to her before putting his arm around her shoulder. "Hey, hey. We came over to cheer you up...not to make you cry?"

I take a step closer to her too, my fucking heart hurting for her. Shit. I hate seeing her like this and I hate the way it makes me feel. Powerlessness is not an emotion I'm used to dealing with but I have no idea how to stop the tears flowing from her beautiful eyes.

Sniffling, Abby wipes quickly at her face, obviously embarrassed. "Just ignore me. I'm sorry guys, it's really sweet of you to stop by and make sure I'm okay. I've just been having a...rough day. You guys can totally stay if you want to." She plops down onto the couch, her arms still wrapped around herself, as if she's trying to make sure she doesn't actually fall to pieces.

"Why don't I get us some glasses?" Jared suggests.

"Or beer. You've got a beer, right?" I ask Abby.

She nods and points to the bottle of wine before pulling it out of the bag. "I'll just take this off your hands," she says and then bursts into shaky sounding laughter. If wine is what Abi needs to put a smile back on her face, I'll buy her a whole damn case.

It only takes a minute for Jared's return from her little kitchen with a corkscrew for Abi and a beer for both of us. Abby wastes no time taking a huge swig from the bottle herself.

I crack open my beer, figuring there's no better way to forget the shittiness in life than to drown it out with some good ol' booze, although I can see Jared's fighting his inner conscience. I can almost hear the little angel and devil sitting on his shoulders, trying to give him advice on how to deal with Abi.

"Maybe we should put something on to watch?" Abby suggests, already searching for the remote to the TV.

"I think there's a good new standup comedy special we could check out," I say. On the other side of Abby, Jared snorts. "Unless you have some lame, boring suggestion, bro."

Jared rolls his eyes at me. "There's this really interesting docudrama about — "

"Docudrama?"

Abi snorts at our banter.

"It's about the world of MMA fighting, Jamie."

I'm just about to interject again when smacks us both on the knees. "You know you guys fight like an old married couple."

I snort back at her this time. "Jared is a bit like an old man, I guess."

"That must make you the old woman then."

Abi's in the middle of taking a swig from the wine bottle and almost spurts out a mouthful.

"Nothing feminine about me," I laugh.

"Me and Cody had been fighting a lot too," Abi says thoughtfully. "I guess I thought it was because of the pressure of organizing the engagement...I guess I missed all the signs."

This isn't exactly the kind of territory I had in mind when I was thinking of cheering our stepsister up. "Better get the docudrama on, Jared," I say and we settle in to watch the exciting world of MMA. It doesn't take long for before everything is reminding Abigail of her former douche bag fiancée in some way. One guy had a haircut exactly like Cody's, while one of the coach's name was actually Cody. It's like she can't get away from the mother fucker. It's one thing for Abi to be upset over the situation, but not when she starts blaming herself for that scumbag's problems.

After more than half the bottle is gone, Abi's freckled cheeks are as red as tomatoes, and she speaks more confidently, sounding surer of the situation and herself. "I've just been so stupid, you know? I mean I knew it was a bit of a stretch when Cody first wanted to start dating. He was the captain of the school's lacrosse team, and I was just some nerdy English major." She gets louder. "I mean really, just take the two of us and compare us side-by-side. Why would someone like Cody want me, anyway?"

I twist to look at her, thinking that maybe she's gonna laugh at the joke she just told but she's starting at the floor morosely. Is she being serious? For fuck sake. I don't want to hear her talk about herself like this. She's beautiful and it just makes me even more fucking angry at Cody for making her feel this way.

"Abi, now you're talking stupid," Jared says in an unusually stern voice for him. "Cody has shit for brains and you need to stop talking badly about yourself."

Abi shakes her head, seemingly having none of it, and tries to stand up, swaying on her feet.

"Yeah, I know you feel like you have to say that…but the reality of the situation is that Cody was out of my league. Simple as that. I'm carrying too much weight, right around here," she says, gesturing to her waist, which I don't understand at all. "And all this mess?" she says, pulling at a thick lock of hair, "it's all coppery and just way too red. I'm nowhere near his usual level of hotness, or whatever you want to call it. He's dated sorority girls in the past. I don't really know how I got him to date me, let alone propose."

I'm just about to say something, my fist balling against my leg when Jared steps in again. "None of that is true, Abi. Like we've told you, and Shay's told you, hell, like everyone's told you… Cody is an idiot. He's a total idiot for leaving you the way he did. And a coward. If he felt like things weren't working out, he should have told you in person instead of letting his friend be the messenger boy. He acted like some kid in middle school, not a grown ass man."

I quickly nod.

"And you know—you know damn well all the rest of it is just in your head. You're beautiful, Abi, and you can have your pick of any guy you want. I guarantee it."

Jared looks at me, something stirring in his eyes that mirror mine, before adding, "…and any of those guys would be totally lucky to have you."

Maybe it's just the fact that I'm on my third beer and it's just starting to kick in, but I sense an interesting shift in the atmosphere of the room. Abi's face flushes hard.

Clearing my throat, I lean forward. "Yeah, I mean you didn't even hear about half the crap we've heard about Cody. Right, Jared?"

My brother nods in agreement, finishing off his third bottle. "Oh yeah. I remember one time we were hanging out at the college bar a couple years ago, I think you guys had been dating for like six months or something maybe, but we saw him at the bar. He was hitting on some of the younger freshmen girls, acting like he wasn't with anyone. When we went over to confront him, he said he was just talking and we were jumping to conclusions but I know what I saw. What an asshole." It takes a lot for Jared to call anyone an asshole, so his feelings on Cody are pretty obvious.

"You think he was cheating?" she asks

Jared glances at me, his eyes wary. "I don't have any evidence of that, hon. If I did, we'd have come and told you what he was doing. There's no way we would have let you marry him. But there were rumors. We thought you would have heard about this from your friends."

Abi shakes her head. "Maybe we could have told you," I say. "But we didn't know anything for sure. I'm not sure what you would have thought or done on the basis of he said, she said."

"And I guess none of it matters now. You see Cody for who he is now, and we know it feels shitty, but time will heal," Jared says. Bloody hell, the guy sounds like Dr. Phil. I want to laugh but it's definitely not an appropriate time. All of this just makes me wonder if I'm ever going to want to get married. It's too much bloody drama. "We just didn't want to ruin anything between you guys. And I mean, look at it this way... You never really know if you're going to piss someone off by telling them something like that, you know what I mean?"

Abi takes a moment, looking as though she's really considering it. "Yeah... I guess you're right. I probably wouldn't have believed you guys if you told me back then. It's still hard to believe, and that's after knowing how crappy he treated me now. I mean I even have my own friends telling me how they didn't trust Cody, like Bailey and Shay, and I still didn't listen to them. So I probably wouldn't have listened to either of you, either. When my friends tried to tell me that they didn't trust him I went without speaking to either of them for a whole week. That was on me...that was really stupid."

"We're all human. We all make dumbass mistakes, it's just kind of part of life, I think. Take it from someone who makes a shit-ton of mistakes on the daily," I say with a grin, popping open the next beer, and clinking it against the wine bottle in Abi's hands.

Abi smiles at me, taking another swig of her drink. "But you know what? Fuck Cody," she says with added emphasis on the fuck. I let out a low whistle, almost wanting to joke on the fact that she never swears.

"Yeah, fuck him," Jared adds, the alcohol obviously getting to him, too.

An immediate grin spreads across Abi's face as she holds up the bottle of wine in the air. "I'm officially starting a new chapter in my life. You're looking at the new and improved Abigail! No more pathetic people-pleaser Abi, No. I'll do what I want when I want. I need to appreciate the things I have in this life, you know? I mean I've got this awesome apartment..." she says, gesturing around the room. "I've got this delicious bottle of wine." She takes another sip, relishing it slowly. "I've got great friends and family..."

At this, Abi leans against Jared's shoulder, squeezing him, looking dazed but still bubbly at the same time. Jared shoots me a curious look as if to say what's going on? I shrug my shoulder at him. She's just drunk. That's all it is.

I no sooner think this to myself than Abi leans closer into Jared, nuzzling against his chest before tilting her face upward, and positioning her mouth over his, kissing him full on the mouth as if it's no big deal.

I shake my head, snapping to reality. What the hell just happened? Jared's surprise expression tells me he's just as shocked as I am, but his eyes flutter shut the next time her lips hover over his, and I can tell that he's no longer shocked and maybe enjoying himself just a bit too much. Fucking hell. I want to shove him out of the way and take his place as her hands grasp at Jared's biceps. I'm not sure what to do but what I do know is that Abi must be wasted and I don't want her to do anything she'll regret in the morning.

"Whoa, whoa. I think maybe the wine got to you, Abi," I say with a chuckle, trying to smooth it over as I break them apart gently.

"Not the wine," she murmurs gently, her eyes moving lazily from Jared's to mine.

I don't believe her, though. My stepsister Abi has never given me any indication that she has feelings for Jared. Well, I mean, I have noticed the way she stared when we were all at the beach. Her complexion doesn't exactly hide when she's flushing either, but I just figured she's a little nervous around us still. Now she's kissing my brother and looking at me as though she wants to lick me like a lollipop on a hot summers day.

Damn.

Ever since that first day I saw her in the restaurant our parents had arranged for us to meet at for the first time, I've always had a thing for pretty little Abi. She doesn't know how gorgeous she is. All those sweet freckles over her nose and her creamy skin that looks so soft. And those curves. I like my women to be women; wide hips and round asses. Thinking about her thighs and what it would be like to be held between them has kept me awake at night.

"Jamie," she sighs, leaning towards me, her gaze trained on my lips.

Fuck. I know I know this is fucked up. This is rebound sex for sure, spurred on by a little too much of what's in that bottle still clutched in her hand. I know I shouldn't be letting her brush her soft lips against mine. I shouldn't be savoring her warmth and the taste of sweet wine that's still fresh on her lips.

But I am.

I'm an asshole for this. I know it but my brain's already fuzzy from the booze, and my conscience is silenced by the pounding of my heart and the raging of my hormones. My hands don't feel like my own as they trail up her shoulders, holding Abi in place as I kiss her back, coaxing open her mouth to taste more of her. The smell of her soft, coppery hair around the both of us is enough to do me in, and as I close my eyes I can hear the couch squeak as Jared moves behind her

I think he's going to pull her away from me as I did before but she keeps on kissing me and when Abi eventually draws back it's not because of my brother. Abi tips the bottle in my direction, waving it around with a grin. I look over her shoulder at Jared and his eyebrows have practically hit the ceiling.

You're probably thinking that we should be offended by Abi's behavior. First, she kisses one of us, then the other. That's not normal behavior. Except it's not a first for me and Jared. It's not a second or a third either.

What can I tell you? There is just something so fucking raw and real about sharing a girl with my brother. I guess we just got used to playing together when we were kids and it carried on into adulthood.

But this isn't just any girl. This is Abi. This is our stepsister. And as much as I want to just let her carry on with what she started, I can't be that guy. Even if I could, I know for sure that Jared couldn't.

"Abi," I say softly. "We can't do this, honey."

But when all the light and happiness leaves her face, I know I've made a terrible mistake.

5

JARED

"You don't want to?" Abi says to Jamie.

She's still clutching the bottle and there's a quiver in her voice that doesn't sound like it's from the drink. I feel for my brother because this is not an easy situation. Abi is drunk. She must be, and even if she's not, she's definitely still reeling from the Cody situation. We can't take advantage of her.

She turns from my brother to me as though she wants to hear it from me too.

"Abi, honey. You've been drinking."

"Yes," she says slowly. Her face is blank and I don't like it one bit.

"And you're still upset from what happened."

"Yes," she says again. "So you think because I've had a few gulps of wine and I'm a bit emotional, that I can't make a decision?"

"It's not that…"

Abi cuts me off with her hand. "You know, Jared. I think, for the first time in a long time, I'm actually thinking crystal clear. This is my life. I get to make the decisions about what I do and don't do. If I want to drink until I'm giddy and have some fun, why should that be something forbidden?" She takes another swig from the bottle, looking thoughtful. "You don't want to, do you? You don't find me attractive."

"What?" Jamie spits. "How the fuck can you say something like that?"

She turns to him but doesn't respond. My mind it blurry from the alcohol but I'm still lucid enough to get what this is. Abi needs to feel desired. She needs to feel like the gorgeous, sexy woman that she is, and the fact that she's chosen me and Jamie makes my heart swell. She trusts us not to hurt her.

I put my hand on her shoulder and turn her. "We want to, Abi," I say softly. "You don't know how much we want to. But are you sure."

She nods, her eyes a little wet as though my words have touched her in some way. She takes two more long swigs from the wine bottle as though she needs the liquid courage, then leans forward to kiss me gently. Abi's lips are so soft, her breath sweet from the wine. I feel intoxicated when she draws away to do the same to Jamie. When she stands and takes both our hands, a shy smile on her face I can't actually get my head around the fact that this is actually happening. I mean, it's not as though I haven't thought about it before. I've practically worn out my brain I've thought about it so much. In all the times I imagined this very thing, none of them had this blur around the edges, or this unreal feeling rushing through my veins.

I don't need to look at Jamie to know what he's thinking because I'm thinking it too. It's really happening. It's really happening.

"Whoa," Jamie mutters as Abi pulls away from us, stroking at the stubble across his jaw. He must be thinking the same thing; we had no idea she'd ever be interested in either of us, much less both of us.

Sweeping the coppery strands away from her face, I cup Abi's cheek and smile. Before I know what's happening, my body reacts on its own, and I'm pulling Abi into my arms, bringing my mouth down to hers and drinking her in.

She tastes like warm sweet wine, but the scent of her strawberry shampoo is doing things to my brain. I wrap my hands up in red tangles and curls, dying to get as close to her as I can.

Jamie comes up to us, and Abi pulls away, gasping as I drop my hands to her waist to spin her to face Jamie. There's a soft moan as his hands slide over the round curve of her ass and he kisses her hard.

I still can't get enough of her either, and I move behind her, wrapping my hands up in her thick hair and pulling it away from her neck, giving me full access to the length of soft skin there. I trail my lips across the nape of Abi's neck and down along her shoulder, slowly back up until I'm tracing the point of my tongue around the shell of her ear. Goosebumps stand across her skin, and I can feel her heart racing through her back. She feeling this just as much as we are.

Abi's hand slips back and I let out a sigh as she strokes me through my pants, my cock already straining against the unforgiving denim. I nip at her neck just as Jamie groans in front of us.

"Fuck, Abi," he hisses, her other hand probably busy working on him.

I get the sudden urge to see more of her and lift the hem of her shirt up, pausing when I realize the seriousness of what's going on here. "Are you sure?" I whisper against her ear.

"Don't stop," she whispers back without hesitation. The sound of her voice tinged with arousal gets me even harder, and I pull the shirt over top of her head, revealing a plain pink bra.

Fuck. It's like unwrapping a present at Christmas. She's exactly what I would have asked Santa for if I thought I had a hope in hells chance.

Kissing the skin along her shoulders, I slide the straps down and unhook the back of the bra until it falls away from her.

This time I turn her to face me so that I can get the full view, and man, it does not disappoint.

Abi's chest is flushed pink and she tries to cover herself up nervously almost as an instinct, but I gently push her hands down.

"You're perfect," I say, meaning it.

Jamie gets closer behind her, not wasting a moment, and begins biting at her ear and neck, the soft skin of her belly breaking out in more goosebumps, and her pink nipples standing out in a way that makes my mouth water. I lean down and kiss her again, wanting to taste her and feel the sounds vibrate in her throat as I slip my hand down the front of her sweatpants, past the thin elastic of her panties, cupping her warm pussy.

She squirms against me, her breath erratic as I push against her with the palm of my hand grounding against her pubic bone. I feel the heat radiating from between her legs, even as she opens them slightly, and I can feel how Jamie's slipped his hand behind Abi too, his fingers pushing deep inside her. She moans and I feel it in my cock.

I trail my mouth down to her soft breasts, pressing kisses across them. When I wrap my lips around one of her nipples and suck, she squirms. "Oh," she gasps.

Thinking only of how good I want her to feel, I continue kissing down between her breasts and along her belly until I'm pulling down the pants and matching pink underwear, revealing everything that I've fantasized about for so long.

Jamie's fingers continue to move inside her and she gazes down at me with heavy-lidded eyes as though she's drunk on what we're doing.

I feel the same way. I run my hands up her legs, spreading them a little wider so that I have the access that I need.

I love Abi's red hair. I know she's conscious of it...the way it makes her stand out where ever we go, but I think that just makes her special. The hair between her legs is just as coppery and my cock kicks with anticipation. Abi's shaking like a leaf and I rest my hand on her thigh to steady her.

"I've got you," I whisper before licking up one side of her pussy and down the other, teasing. I can't help but smile against her when her thighs quiver around me, urging me on.

Above me, Jamie's caressing her breasts, whispering how badly he wants to be inside her.

I feel that way too, but first I want to show her how good I can make her feel.

With Jamie preoccupied, I use my fingers to add to her pleasure, curling them up tightly and stroking the little sweet spot that has her gasping.

"Ohhh," she moans quietly, her legs shaking even more.

"Does that feel good?" I look up at her, and etch the way she looks down at me with total lust in her eyes, to my memory forever. "Good," I say, and flick my tongue against the underside of her clit, doing it once, twice. Abi's legs shake so much that I'm sure she's not going to be able to hold back from coming much longer, and just like that, Jamie is backing us up to the couch. He sits her on his lap and spreads her legs wide so that I can get even deeper. Damn. Knowing he's holding her just slightly turns me on so damn much. Her hand comes to my head and I don't disappoint her. With tiny flicks of my tongue, I send her over the edge and it's the most beautiful thing I've ever seen.

"Oh god, oh yes, just like that," she moans even louder this time.

She squeezes her legs around me, desperate, and I give her exactly what she wants. Plunging my fingers deeper inside of her, I stroke her insides faster, circling her clit with my tongue in rhythm.

Abi writhes against my face, her breath coming in pants.

"You like it when he licks your sweet pussy?" Jamie growls, his mouth still on her neck.

She quickly nods and her hips rise off the edge of the couch as if she were possessed. I hold her in place, my mouth sealed against her, tasting her as she lets out one last squeal, "I'm…I'm…I…"

Her body jerks and I work my tongue faster, my fingers pumping in and out of her, helping her reach the climax she deserves.

I'm still in awe as I watch her skin flush a darker pink, her walls close tightly around me, everything about her absolutely perfect. "Beautiful," I mumble against her.

She lies back on Jamie, but we aren't finished yet, and I scoop her up in my arms, carrying her limp body to her bedroom, kicking open the door before laying her down on the bed gently.

She gazes up at me, her pretty eyes dazed, pushing the sweaty strands of hair away from her face.

Jamie stands beside me at the end of the bed.

"Are you okay?" I ask her and she nods.

"Ready for more?" Jamie says. I can hear the grin in his voice. Abi looks between us and I think I see a little uncertainty there, but she nods, biting her lip. I guess maybe it's the fact that there's two of us. I'm pretty sure this is her first time with more than one partner, and I can't forget the relationship we have had over the past few years. What I just did takes us well out of the realms of stepbrother/stepsister into something a whole lot raunchier.

Jamie begins to shuck his clothes and Abi watches. She licks her lips and I know then that she wants this. I loosen my belt and drop my pants, toeing off my socks. When we're both naked, Abi looks pretty stunned. Jamie holds his cock at the root.

"You think you'll be able to handle us?" he asks. It's a fair question. We're definitely at the upper end of the scale when it comes to size.

Abi shakes her head. "You…you're both…"

"Big," Jamie finished for her.

"Huge," she says in awe. Then she burst out laughing. "Are you serious with those?" she slurs nodding at our cocks.

I shake my head at her, kneeling on the bed and make my way towards her. "Nah, we're joking," I whisper in her pretty ear.

Jamie climbs next to her on the other side. "Ignore my brother," he says. "We take our cocks very seriously."

We all chuckle until Abi's hands wrap around both of us at the same time. Her strokes are firm and we moan simultaneously. I'm not expecting her to be as forthright as she is.

"Damn," she mutters. "You don't know how long I've thought about this."

She has?

I glance across at Jamie who raises his eyebrows. I guess it's not only us who've been thinking things that should be forbidden all this time.

I can't keep my hips still. The way she's holding me makes me want to thrust. I can still taste her pussy in my mouth and I want to feel that soft wetness around my dick.

Jamie makes a move to kneel between her legs. I watch him touch her, every caress makes my dick swell until I can't take it anymore. Abi lays back, letting go of my cock and kissing my brother slow and deep. He pulls back and gets himself into position. I watch her face as he works his way inside her; the way her cheeks flush high along her cheekbones and her eyes flutter closed. A soft moan leaves her lips.

"That feel good?" he asks and she nods, then her eyes turn my way, searching.

"Jared," she says.

I make my way closer and she shows me what she wants.

This is what sharing is all about. As much as I want to bury myself inside of her pussy, I can wait and enjoy her mouth.

I let out a hiss as she gently runs her fingers along my balls and tilt my head back, lost in how warm her tongue is as she strokes my rigid cock with it. It's more than I ever thought it could be, and I tangle my hands in her hair just to have something tangible at reach, just to believe that this is really happening.

As she works her perfect mouth up and down my shaft Jamie fucks her. I watch the pleasure on her face and enjoy the way she whimpers around my cock. I notice the signs-the squirming, her cheeks flushing more, and realize she's so close again.

Jamie yells out, releasing deep inside of her, thrusting hard against her one last time.

Determination takes over, and all I can think about is feeling her around me.

As soon as he pulls out of her, I turn and pull her into my lap, not bothering with any words as I sit her squarely down on my cock, her warmth encasing me completely.

I know I won't last long because her mouth felt so good, so I kiss her breasts and hold her close as I fuck her. She moans louder as I get closer, feeling frantic. Abi's head tilts back and I'm already there, the both of us crying out loudly as we come at the same time, my hips holding her in place as I shove deeper. I can't even explain just how perfectly we fit together. All the times I fantasized about this moment have never come close.

Her head droops against my shoulder and I can feel her breath against me. Jamie's moved behind her, and he drops a kiss on the back of her neck.

She wraps her arms around me, holding me like I'm her anchor, but in reality, she's mine.

I don't want to let go of her. Not now, not ever.

6

ABIGAIL

My skin is on fire. It's like being sandwiched inside of a solid furnace, either side of me practically baking under the sheets. Sweat has plastered bits of my hair to my forehead and the nape of my neck, and in my groggy state all I can think about is crawling out of bed and turning the shower on.

But the furnace groans, turning closer against me on one side, and my eyes fly open.

Jared is curled up on my left, while Jamie has his arm tucked up under my head on my right, and neither of them seems to be awake. Yet.

My eyes flutter shut again, and flashes of everything that happened last night permeate my morning brain fog one by one.

I had sex with Jared and Jamie.

I had sex with both of my step-brothers.

It's hard not to hyperventilate in between them like this, slowly realizing what we did. A strange mix of mortification and awe swirls around inside of me, spreading across my nerves like a blanket of beautiful and dangerous buzzing creatures. There's no going back now, not with them lying naked with me in my bed. I carefully peek under the sheets with my free hand. Yep. Definitely very naked.

I remember Jared's hands in my hair, meeting my kisses with the kind of passion that spun my head around...how Jamie ground against me, the sharp jab of his hipbones as his breath ghosted across my bare neck...the way they practically worshipped by body, one fabulous touch after another...

I just had the best sex of my life. With my step-brothers. I reach up and touch my lips in amazement, still kiss-bruised from the action they saw last night. The smile inches across my face briefly, until the reality of the day crushes me in a single fell swoop.

How am I going to live this down? I've never done anything like this before, and there's just no way something this...this big...won't find its way to the light of day.

It takes me a minute to gather my nerves, but I try to edge my way back from Jamie's reach, but end up accidentally backing up into Jared. I freeze in place when his warm brown eyes slowly open, finding mine easily. The lazy smile that spreads across his face is almost enough to keep me here with them, but I know it doesn't work like that, and when Jared leans forward and his soft lips start to brush against mine I have to yank myself away from him.

"No," I mutter, struggling to cover myself up as Jared's eyes drop to my naked breasts. "No, we can't do this."

"Hm?" Jamie mumbles until I can feel his presence looming up behind me, his hand slipping to cup my partially covered hip.

"What's going on, Abi? Are you okay?" Jared asks, sounding genuinely concerned.

I pull myself up to a sitting position, trying my hardest to cover myself up, my cheeks flushed red. "Yes, yes, I'm all right. It's okay. I mean I had a great time with you guys, but y'know. It was a one-off." I'm already scooting up until I'm pinned against the headboard, feeling trapped. "We can't do this again. I mean, we're…"

"Don't say we're family, Abi," Jamie says. There's an edge of annoyance in his voice.

"In our parent's eyes, we are."

"Not in mine," Jamie says.

"Or mine." I turn to Jared and his expression is too hard to read.

No one seems to move. But I need everyone to move, to give me some time to process what all this means and what I need to do now. "I think I need to get a shower and have some time to myself to think about things."

The guys keep looking between me and one another, the gears turning. I nudge at them politely to move out of the way and pull the rest of the sheets up behind me as I start to pick my way over Jamie's solid body, not wanting to wait another second. Another second would have me gawping at how amazing their bodies are. Another second would have me tempted to just slide back between them for another ticket to heaven.

Oh god.

Jamie's brow is furrowed, and I can tell by the way his eyes narrow at me that he wants to argue that I'm wrong so badly. Jared notices too and holds up his hand. "We better get dressed, then," he says calmly. I'd expect nothing less from him.

"I'll give you some privacy," I add, making a beeline to my own bathroom, nearly slamming it shut behind me.

I check out my reflection in the mirror, examining every square inch that I can, looking for something, some kind of sign that I might just be dreaming this whole thing up. But I'm real. This is real. I groan, cradling my head in my hand as I lean up against the bathroom counter cluttered with makeup.

"Oh God, Abigail," I moan to myself, "What did you get yourself into?" I'm a fraud, though, because I remember being the one to kiss them first. I remember telling them that it was exactly what I wanted and needed. I remember being the one who started it all.

Slipping on my sweatpants and a gym shirt still doesn't do enough to keep me from feeling so overexposed when I step out of the bathroom. With both of their backs turned away from me, carrying on a heated argument via whispering, Jared and Jamie give me a full view of their toned backs, the wide arcs of their shoulders tapering down to chiseled and well-defined obliques that even my personal trainer would be jealous over. I had those marbled smooth bodies under my hands last night, exploring them both every chance I had. I never realized they had it in them the way they seduced me. Jamie, sure, but the quiet and careful touch of Jared balanced out Jamie's brash fiery personality. Truth be told, they were amazing in bed, more than I could have hoped for. All they wanted to do was to please me. I've never experienced anything like it.

My mind blurs some of the images together because of the wine, and I stumble as I nearly trip over the pile of dirty clothes on the floor. Both Jared and Jamie turn and face me at the same time, and I have to steel myself from the feelings that tumble around inside me. It's the expressions on their faces. I want to go to them, to make it right, but that's the very last thing I should be doing.

"You have to swear not to tell anyone what happened between us," I blurt out loud, immediately clapping my hand over my mouth. I shouldn't have said that because I know they wouldn't. They're good men. Not like Cody and his friends, bragging all the time about who they fucked with all the details.

Even so, no one can find out about this, especially not our parents. The thought of my dad finding out leaves my skin feeling itchy and tight. "I'm sorry…I know you won't tell anyone," I add, taking in a deep breath, "but no one can know."

Jamie's eyes go wide, giving him away, but Jared keeps the same cool expression on his face.

"Of course," he says, nodding slowly. With a nudge in his brother's direction, he adds, "We should probably be going."

Stupid tears well up in my eyes as I pull my arms across my chest and give him a quick nod, watching as the two of them leave. I can hear Jamie muttering something to Jared but can't quite make out what he's saying. Whatever it is, it doesn't sound good.

Once I hear the front door shut behind them, I stare around my room, feeling like I need to do something, anything, to get rid of this feeling. I pushed things too far. It was me, and then I hurt their feelings in the process. They've always been there for me in some way or another, and here I am, taking all that for granted.

I used them. That's how it feels.

When my body finally starts to feel like my own again, I tidy up the bedroom, trying not to imagine an overlay of last night's events. Jared's wide grin as he laid me down on the bed here, Jamie's shirt being tossed over the back of the chair there. I run my hand along the length of my other arm, imagining for a split second that I was allowed to do these things with them, and that no one would bat an eye in my direction. I bite my lip and sigh. The truth is that there's no point in pretending. It only makes things worse.

As I'm fixing the sheets on the bed, I get a whiff of them, the clean scent of their soap and the hair gel Jared uses to tame down his hair, and something saltier. The scent of pure sex.

Something twinges inside of me, but not in a good way. I think back to right before I felt Jamie inside me, trying to recall what happened in the moments before. Kissing. Touching. A lot more of Jared than I'd ever seen or felt before. And then…what?

Oh no. Oh no, oh no. My mouth goes dry.

We didn't use protection. Neither of them put on condoms, and with me not being on birth control since the last pill made me feel sick there was no barrier between me and them.

My stomach roils as I collapse to the bed, holding my head in my hands. All this, topped off with a wonderful hangover, no less.

"FUCK!" I shout, so unlike myself and more like some angry teen, balling my fists into the sheets and mattress. I can't let myself think about that. It will only drive me crazy, all that watching and waiting. Besides, it had only been once, right? I roll my eyes at myself. Sure, once. As in one night, total. There had been plenty of chances after the first time Jamie and then Jared was inside of me.

I think back to the way the guys greeted me with lazy smiles this morning, seeming so at ease and relaxed. Hadn't I felt that way too, at first? I could have just let myself be in the moment for now, and enjoy it before I have to get back to the real world.

The way they made me feel last night. My god, I've never felt that way before. Like every nerve in my body was being tuned to a frequency that shot me off into the stars.

It wasn't just the way their thick, muscular bodies moved against mine in perfect synchronization, or even how utterly full and complete I felt between the two of them as they had their way with me over and over again. It was the things they whispered against my skin. It was in the way Jared curled his fingers behind my neck and looked me straight in the eyes, and in the way Jamie took his time exploring every inch of my body with his mouth, never rushing. They treated me like an absolute queen, and I loved it.

Even in the drunken haze that clouds some of the finer details, I can remember thinking how amazing it all was, how I never wanted any of it to stop. I smile in spite of myself, looking out the window.

But like a sledgehammer to a concrete block, guilt breaks over me as I think about what something like this could do to our family. What if something like this ruined our parent's relationship?

Neither Jared, Jamie, or I would ever want to do that to them, and I would be hard-pressed to find any two people more in love than my dad and Natalie.

I roll away from the window and the light pouring in, feeling too many ways to properly process. Just as my eyes feel too heavy to keep open, regret sinks into my brain. Regret that I don't live in the kind of world where I could see where whatever this thing between the three of us might lead.

7

JARED

I lean back on my heels, inspecting the lineup of the piping. The last time I was here at Miranda's place, her six-year-old, Cassie, had managed to gunk up the kitchen sink with some homemade slime concoction. This time it's a backed-up garbage disposal.

I inspect it one more time, just to be sure, and flip the switch by the sink, turn on the faucet and let both run, listening to the loud whirring. Everything seems good now. Simple enough fix.

I didn't have to take the extra job today but to be honest I needed the distraction. after the way everything went down with Abi a few days ago, it's all I can do to keep my focus off of her.

The back-door creaks open, and I see a little gap-toothed smile and a pair of big blue eyes watching me.

"All right. Let's have it."

Cassie comes bounding in, her blonde ponytail swinging behind her. I move away from the sink and let her get a good look, unable to stop myself from cracking a smile even as she walks slowly around me with a staged serious expression on her face.

"Hmm," she says, tapping her chin. All she needs is a pipe and a detective's cap. "You're wearing the same shirt as always. It's too hard to tell. Can you say something again?"

"Something again." I grin.

"Uh!" Cassie pretends to stomp her foot down. "It's not fair. You sound the same, too!"

I lean down until we're almost eye level. "But if you had to guess…"

"Jamie?" she replies half-hopefully.

"Nope, try again," I wink at her.

"Did he stump you again?" Miranda asks, coming in from the backyard as well.

I stand back up and wipe my hands on my rag and point to the open cabinets under the sink. "All fixed."

Cassie huffs. "I never know which one you are!"

"Don't feel bad, Cassie. My own mom doesn't always know which one I am, either," I tell her, closing the cabinet doors.

"Bet my mom knows which one you are," she mumbles back, her arms folded across her chest.

"That's because I'm the one footing the bill," Miranda replies, tickling under Cassie's arm until she grins at her again.

"Thanks for coming out on such short notice. Again," she sighs, shaking her head.

Maybe it's just because I know what it's like being raised by a tough single mom, but I always like coming by to work for Miranda. She's never given me too much information about her and Cassie's situation, and I don't pry, but I can tell she can get frustrated, especially when me or Jamie are needed. There's an always present strain in her eyes, and as much as I would never admit it to her, she reminds me a lot of my mom.

"What's the damage?" she asks, putting on her reading glasses as I hand her the clipboard.

"The usual," I reply, shrugging. Another thing I would never admit to Miranda? Both me and Jamie always give her a discount just because. And we don't tell her because we both know she'd never allow it.

"Oh, I almost forgot!" I fish around in my bag for the lollipop I made sure to grab on the way over. "Blueberry this time." I hand it to Cassie who immediately cheers up a thousand percent, beaming like crazy up at me. "Thank you!"

She throws her arms around me and I gently pat her head. Out of the corner of my eye, I see Miranda watching, her face softening.

"You know, you'll make a really great dad, someday," she says thoughtfully, adding her signature with a flourish to the bottom of the worksheet. "Jamie too, even."

"Now you're pushing it," I chuckle. We both know how stubborn and well, Jamie-like, my brother can be.

"No, no, I mean it. You seem to have a way with kids. You should be proud of that. Not all men are like that."

I pretend not to notice the sadness in her voice.

Things were the same for a while with Mom. I know that she had it rougher than she'd ever care to admit to me or Jamie, and that's the main reason why instead of getting all way-overprotective of her, we were relieved when she found Keith.

Well, at least we were after a while, anyway; when he'd proved himself to be worthy of her.

Cassie tugs on my sleeve. "Are you going to come back the next time? Or is it going to be Jamie?"

"Are you asking me to cheat and give you the answer? I don't think so. Besides..." I add with a laugh, "...as long as you don't try any more experiments on the kitchen sink, your mom can take care of things pretty well on her own."

Miranda's face brightens a little as she hands over her credit card. "One can only hope."

I thank her, waving bye to her and Cassie, and head out the front door, satisfied.

Maybe it was Miranda's words about me being a good dad, or maybe it was goofing around with Cassie, but I feel good. I have to chuckle at the thought of what my mom would say, and whether she'd agree with Miranda. I can't imagine being a dad yet, but someday it's definitely my plan.

I'm missing one pretty fundamental factor, though; someone to have a baby with.

Just like that, Abi's pretty face comes back in view.

I feel like a kid who got given his favorite toy for Christmas and then had it snatched away. It was hard before I knew what it felt like to be with her. Now I know, I can't stop thinking about her. The worst thing is that I have no idea how she really feels. I thought...or hoped that she was as into us as we are into her, but then she pushed us away like we'd just made the most terrible mistake.

Jamie's as confused about it as me. I can't really say I know what's going through her head. I wish I did.

I check my watch, surprised to see how much of the day has already passed by. It wouldn't hurt to just stop by, would it?

I throw my bag over my shoulder, resolving to go over and check on Abi once I'm done. She might not want a repeat of the best night of my life, but that doesn't mean I can be her friend. Maybe, just maybe, she might have changed my mind. I guess, one way or the other, I'll have my answer soon enough.

8

JAMIE

"Hey thanks, Paul. I owe you one."

I hit the end button on my phone and lean back in my seat, watching the cars go by.

Maybe I should feel guilty about dropping out of work early for the day, but I'm so damn distracted by all things Abigail-related, that I nearly left a stupid snake in one of the s-bends of a client's toilet.

"You gotta get your head on straight, man," I say to my reflection in the rearview, running my hand through my hair. I yank it away the moment Abi's gorgeous red hair springs back into my head like an all-out fucking assault on my senses, my pride, and not to mention my dick. I adjust myself accordingly before throwing the truck into drive.

I know the moment that I park, I'm not going inside just yet. Abi's car is in the apartment complex's parking lot, and I chew on my lip, debating. With all that went down between the three of us that night and then Abi wigging out the next morning, I haven't had much of a chance to say anything to her. Jared begged me not to go 'making things worse,' by trying to talk to her, but who would I be, listening to my little brother's every wish like that?

"Fuck it."

I stride across the street, stopping to make sure my breath isn't gross after my lunch, and knock on her door.

I don't hear anything inside, so I knock louder this time and wait. I'm not exactly known for being the patient type. I mentally try and go over what I want to say to her, how I want to apologize—something I don't ever do. But my brother's sorta right…I don't want to make things worse and I have a shitty way with words sometimes.

From somewhere inside, I hear Abi's voice calling out.

Not long after, the door opens, so I launch into my whole spiel as fast as I can. "The thing is Abi, I'm not sorry about what happened with us, but I am seriously sorry that it made you feel uncomfortable because that's not what we meant to do—"

She's in front of me, her t-shirt half-soaked and her face red from exertion, brandishing a large wrench, staring at me as if she's seeing a ghost. It's a funny enough scene that if I weren't in the middle of apologizing, I would probably laugh.

I raise an eyebrow at her. "Busy?"

Abi blows a strand of hair from her face. "You could say that. I've been working on this stupid sink for over half-an-hour. I can seem to fix the little doohickey."

Snorting, I let myself inside. "Doohickey, huh? You might want to let me handle that since I'm—you know—the professional and all." I can practically feel her eyes rolling as I head further in. "Lead the way, ma'am."

She may try to hide it, but there's definitely a smile on her face as she scoots past me and heads to the bathroom. "It's back here. I busted my butt in here because the floor was flooded with nearly an inch of water around the sink. I thought maybe there was a leak somewhere, but I'm not sure."

Sure enough, there's water all around the base of the sink, and wet towels pushed into the corner of the room. When Abi turns toward the sink I even see where she fell ass-first into the water, the liquid leaving a heart-shaped print on her fine behind. Not the time...not the time.

My dick doesn't seem to be listening.

"All right, let me take a look here," I say, leaning down and checking out the pipes underneath. "Oh yeah, I can already see it. It looks like there's a hairline crack along the length of the trap here." I point to the small crack that's leaking a few drops at a time. "It's a pretty easy fix."

"The trap?"

"This part right here, you see the pipe? That's the trap."

Abi leans down close enough for me to smell the sweet scent of her hair, her face screwed up in concentration as she looks for the crack. "Oh. Okay, I see it. So, the big pipe is the trap?"

I smirk, unable to help myself. "Some think so."

Just as I hoped, Abi's cheeks flush pink. She leans away from me and runs her fingers over the leak. "What could've caused something like this? It's not like I shove a lot of stuff in there."

Oh, she makes it too easy. "Shoving things into your pipe isn't all that bad sometimes…but yeah," I continue, turning back to the sink, "this is definitely going to need to be replaced."

"Well, I mean, I didn't mean like—" she sputters, but I just wave her off.

"It's okay, Abi, I know what you meant. I think I actually have a few extra replacement trap pipes that will fit here. If you give me a minute, I can go run and get them from my truck." I don't stick around for the reply, knowing she'll probably just say something stupid about not needing my help—the typical Abi reply. God knows she doesn't want anyone thinking she can't handle something herself.

When I come back inside I notice how she's taken her hair down from the bun it was in, and it takes me all of the focus I can muster not to stare at it.

"Could you grab me a—"

"Here you go," she says, sticking a hand towel into my open palm.

I nod feeling a little awkward at how eerie it is that she's guessed exactly what I was going to say. "Ah, okay. Cool."

"Is it hard?"

I laugh because it has been since I saw her are the door, but I don't think she was referring to that. I bend down to get under the sink.

Abi chuckles a little, groaning. "I meant, is it difficult. Trying to fix the leak in the pipe?" she gestures to the sink.

"Nah, it's not that bad. You just have to make sure the pipe is cut to fit right, and that you have enough caulk to fill it up. Goddamn," I sigh, shaking my head at myself when Abi bursts out laughing. "You've got a dirty mind, you know that?"

She feigns being offended. "Uh! I so don't. It's you! You're a bad influence!"

I turn off the water valve, still looking at her. "What can I say? I've always been the naughty one. Mom could tell you some stories."

I get hold of the tool I need. "Okay, so I'm going to take this part off here…"

I spend the next hour replacing the old pipe with a new one, and I may have taken twice as long to replace Abi's pipe just because. "Ouch. Stiff back," I say, finally standing up. "But it's all done, at least. As long as you're not shoving things down your drain, you shouldn't have a problem."

Abi rolls her eyes but she's smiling and I fucking love to see it.

She's trying to put things back on a level with us and I don't question it. It's why I came round to check on her in the first place. I don't want to move from where I am but I have to. Abi awkwardly leads me from the bathroom, clearing her throat when I head to the door. "Hey, uh, thanks, Jamie."

Dammit. Why does she have to always pull me back like this? "You're welcome. It's not a big deal, really." Abi digs into the wallet that's on the table, and when I realize what she's trying to do, I put my hand over hers, shaking my head when she meets my eyes again. "You don't have to pay me, seriously. Listen, Abi, I wanted to tell you I'm sorry."

"For what?"

"You know. I didn't want you to be uncomfortable the other night. I'm just sorry, that's all."

Fuck, I'm beginning to sound like Jared.

Abi's face softens and she goes quiet for a minute. "Don't be sorry," she says. "I'm not sorry it happened, Jamie. It just can't happen again."

It's the words I didn't want to hear, and they sting just as hard the second time.

"Okay," I say. "You call me if you need anything, okay. Plumbing related or not."

She smiles. "I will."

I wave as I walk away. After a few steps I turn back and she's still standing at the door watching me leave and I have no idea what to make of that.

9

ABIGAIL

After getting washed up from the earlier sink fiasco, I finally have a chance to settle in and see how much I made this past week at Dandie's. Anything to get my mind off the way Jamie came in like my knight and shining armor.

"Well, at least I'll be able to buy some decent groceries this week. Who knows? Maybe I'll even splurge and pick up a couple new shirts." I let out a small sigh of relief, just grateful that I'm able to still stand on my own two feet without Cody here pretending to have my back.

There's a tap on my door and I quickly turn around in my seat, wondering who the heck could be visiting this time. Shay's with her family and Bailey's out of town now. Unless my dad is doing a random drop-in, maybe. He doesn't usually surprise me but I know he's worried.

Learning from earlier, I check the peephole. Jared.

It takes me a moment to compose myself before I throw open the door with a little too much enthusiasm. "Hey, uh, what are you doing here?"

"I just wanted to come by and check in with you. You know, to make sure you're feeling okay. The way we left things before was a little, uh, abrupt," he replies, cutting right to the point. Well, at least he's honest.

I can feel the heat rising in my cheeks. "Oh. Right." I shouldn't let my feelings get so twisted up in my chest every time he speaks, but it's sort of hard not to. Realizing I'm staring at him, I bite my lip and move over. "Sorry. Come in."

The truth is that I don't want to have any kind of conversation with Jared about what happened. The more I think about that night and what we did, the harder it is to stop thinking about it.

He walks past and waits for me by the couch, his eyes never leaving mine. "I just wanted to know that we're okay. Are we? Okay?"

"Yeah, why wouldn't we be?" My way too casual tone isn't fooling anyone.

"You're not mad at us, are you?"

This, I wasn't expecting. Mad. Is that what they think. "I'm not mad, Jared. Not at all. What happened…it's not like I didn't want to, you know?" I say more to myself than to Jared.

He nods. "I just had to make sure we didn't make you mad because that would not have sat well with me or Jamie. We just want you to be happy."

Warmth spreads through my veins like a slow-burning flame. Why does Jared have to be so sweet and caring all the time? It would definitely make it easier to avoid thinking about him if he wasn't.

"I appreciate that," I say softly. "I'm okay. We're good."

"Good." He beams at me and I practically melt on the spot. "And…if you ever need anything, anything at all, Abi, just tell me. Just let me know."

I sigh gently. "Thanks, Jared." The contrast between the way my stepbrothers treat me and Cody is just so stark and it feels completely unfair. They make me feel so safe and secure and Jared, in particular, has always had this presence around him that leaves me calmer. I let his words roll around in my head

What I need is to feel him inside of me again, holding me close, taking his time with me until I feel the ultimate release. My eyes widen as the thought. I need to stop before my fantasies start spiraling out of control. I lick my lips quickly and turn back to him. "I good right now, Jared. I really need to get back to my, ah, cooking. Or it'll burn."

Jared twists until he's sniffing for the non-existent food in the kitchen. "Oh really? What are you making?"

Without missing a beat, I walk over to the front door and open it, smiling at him the best that I can. "Soup. Some plain, boring soup. I didn't even really want it, but I needed to go ahead and eat it while I still can."

He seems to take the hint, and nods, smiling at me. "I'll leave you to it, then. Just remember…let me know." He ends this with a knowing look that I have to glance away from. There's just no way I can keep staring up at him without letting all my feelings out in the process.

"I will."

Jared gives me one more nod before walking out and letting me shut the door. My chest loosens a little, finally able to relax. When did it become such a physically impossible venture to let the guys leave?

Probably when you basically seduced them, the other side of me chimes in, reminding me. And maybe I'm right. Maybe I was just feeling bad about myself and only wanted their attention without their affection. It's definitely possible.

My chest tightens yet again at the thought of this. I don't want to lead my step-brothers on, but I don't know if this is me leading them on, or if this is me wanting my deepest desires to be real again.

10

JARED

With Abigail still on my mind, I'm feeling a little less worried and a little more thoughtful about things as I take and park my car back over at our place. When I see Jamie's truck already sitting outside the house, I have to do a double take. Inside, he is on the couch, beer in hand and watching me as I come in the door.

"What are you doing back so late?" he asks, raising a brow in my direction.

I snort. "Me? What? What about you... Why are you home so early? It's Friday night, isn't it? Aren't you usually out you know...doing things on Friday night?" At least that's how it's always been, up until recently, but I keep this part to myself.

My brother's eyes narrow at me. "It's been a while since I've picked up some chick from the bar, Jared. Or haven't you noticed."

I figure biting the bullet and getting this over with is probably the best way to handle things with him. "I wanted to talk to you about Abi," I say, sitting down on the opposite end of the couch, leaning forward.

Jamie sorts, "What's there to talk about...we fucked up thinking that she wanted anything other than rebound sex."

I nod. "Yeah. It's complicated."

"Complicated? Nah...more like a cluster fuck."

I roll my eyes because Jamie can't seem to communicate without f-bombing all over the place. "Yeah, you're right. It's definitely a cluster-fuck. Normally I really wouldn't care but..."

"...but this is Abi," Jamie says nodding.

"Exactly." I let my voice trail off, thinking of how Abi acted when I was at her apartment; flustered and cool at the same time, obviously trying to sort out her own feelings.

The other women I've shared with my brother have been those usual wild, I-want-to-fuck-you-because-you're-twin-brothers, kind of girls. But not Abi. She is pretty much the literal translation of girl-next-door material. Wholesome, family oriented. Abi is so much, but it doesn't make this conversation with my own twin brother any less awkward.

I rub my hand across my brow, trying to work out how to approach what I want to say. "Yeah, yeah. I get it. Before, with the others...we didn't really have to say anything after, did we? The thing is, it's different with Abi, and things are blurrier in my mind than I'd like to admit, I guess. You don't think…I mean we didn't…"

"I don't know what you're about to say, but I swear to God, Jared, if you even mention touching junk, I will come across this couch and punch you square in the goddamn jaw. I swear I will."

"That wasn't what I was going to say."

"Thank fuck for that." My brother picks up his phone and started replying to a message. He has a stupid smirk on his face. "It was good though, right? Like, really, really good."

I let out a low whistle. "You are not lying," I agree. "I mean I have a few moments where it's a little less detailed, and maybe a little bit hazier than I'd like, but it was really good."

Jamie quickly nods along in agreement, turning back toward me. "When you've wanted something for so long and you finally get it…I mean…damn." He shakes his head.

"Yeah…when she kissed me first, I didn't know what to do."

Jamie snorts. "She only kissed you first because you were closest. She got hotter quicker when she kissed me."

"Yeah, because you practically pulled her off me…didn't think you'd be so jealous, man."

"Jealous? Get outta here," he laughs. "I thought she was too drunk to know what she was doing. I was trying not to let you damage our sibling relationship."

I punch Jamie's leg. "Number one, she was kissing me, not the other way around and number two we are not siblings."

"You know what I mean, and it sure looked like you were kissing her back."

"Yeah well, you didn't exactly push her away when she turned her attentions to you."

Jamie chuckles lowly. "What do you expect…I'm a man, not a monk."

"Look, we're going around in circles here," I say. It's weird because we never really get jealous over the other girls we've shared.

Jamie seems to understand at the same time that I do, that there's just no point in any of the arguing. "The point is she had a good time, and that's what matters," he says, putting a cap on the obvious dick-measuring.

The fact that Jamie is the one to stop it, though, still kind of stuns me. "Yeah. Yeah, you're right. That's all that should matter."

"But seriously, bro, we didn't touch junk, did we?"

I give him a hard shove. "Fuck off, Jamie."

He laughs hard and punches my arm. "Jared, did you just say fuck?"

"It must be catching." I shrug but smile back at my brother. For all our petty sibling bickering, I love my twin like nothing else.

He hands me a beer and I grab the bottle opener from his other hand and pop it open, taking a swig.

"All right. So we had sex with Abi, and it was really good. The best, but now we achieved the dream, it's over and done with. Right? She's made that clear." It stings little to say it, but I have to know that were both on the same page. Neither one of us should be pursuing her. Especially since it doesn't seem to be what she wants.

"She's told us how she feels about what happened and I guess we have to respect that. I don't like it but what can I do."

I nod. As much as we would both jump at the opportunity to have more with Abi, it doesn't look like either of us is going to get another chance.

11

JAMIE

"Ugh, does the bastard ever put shit away?" I mumble to myself, sifting through the junk and remaining parts Jared's left in the mud room. He has a bad tendency of emptying out his work van here instead of tidying it up. I've been looking for his spare rotary tool for the last five minutes and still haven't come across the damn thing yet.

Underneath some more junk, I lean back when I unearth a brand-spanking new garbage disposal kit still sealed in the box. Damn, is this the one that we lost a couple of months ago? It had driven us both crazy looking for it, and we had to eventually turn around and order a replacement kit, prolonging our customer's wait, which royally pissed me off, and didn't exactly make them happy.

"Well, what the hell am I going to do with you now?" I wonder aloud as if the thing is going to talk back to me or something. I groan. "I'm losing my mind now, I guess."

It hits me that while I was at Abi's apartment last time, I grabbed some water and noticed that she didn't seem to have a working garbage disposal. When I asked her about it, she mentioned that while there was supposed to be one connected to her sink's plumbing, the apartment manager never got around to putting a new one in. *"It would probably be a really cheap one anyway, so I never saw the point in bringing it back up. It's not like I really need it."*

Maybe it's time to put this box to use, after all. No harm in keeping relations friendly, I think. What I mean is that I'm craving a fix of Abi. Even if all I get is a look at her and a little easy chatter it'll be enough to keep me happy.

And no one's going to miss this part now!

--

It takes some doing, but I manage to finish up at my last client's home and immediately hop into my truck and throw it into drive, heading home, or to Abi's, I should say.

When I'm there I turn off the ignition and sit for a minute. I think about how fucking happy I was when she pressed her lips against mine. She has no idea how much I've wanted her all these years. Seeing her with Cody about killed me, but I wasn't in any position to fight for her. I just had to sit back and watch her put all her hopes and dreams into someone who didn't deserve to breathe the same air as her, let alone put a ring on her finger.

I know I shouldn't be here right now. I did the 'breaking the ice' visit already. Things are as cool between us as it's possible for them to be under the circumstances. I'm not going to make anything better but popping over again so soon, but I can't help myself. I just want to see her. I feel better when I'm in her presence; calmer...less angry. I can't bear to see her unhappy. As soppy as it sounds, I just want to put my arms around her and shelter her from all the shit that life has to throw in her direction.

I know that dropping by to fit this waste disposal is stupid, but I don't care. As I get out of the truck, I look up at her window, hoping that she's home. I shoulder the box and carry it across the street to her apartment complex, careful watch where I'm going, before ringing her doorbell.

The door opens and Abi's there wearing a pleased expression on her face, along with a rather low-cut tank-top and gray yoga pants. Bless whoever brought those into style.

"Hey! I was actually just about to text you to thank you for fixing my sink…I wasn't sure if I told you that or not." Abi pauses, finally taking in the box. "What's that?" she asks, eyeing it warily.

"Oh, uh, I wanted to stop by and see if you would like me to hook this up for you." I point to the side of the box. "It's a garbage disposal for your kitchen sink."

Abi moves aside to let me in. "Well, I mean, okay. It's really not a big deal. I don't ever put anything down the drain…okay, you're really doing this." She hurries to follow me into her small kitchen.

Dropping down to one knee, I pull the cabinets open. "Yeah, it won't be too hard to replace this piece of shit you got in here already. Promise," I reply, ripping the top of the box off. "Besides, that asshole landlord of yours should've already had this done, right?"

"Yeah. Yeah, it was supposed to be done months ago," she says, holding her herself together for some reason. "And this isn't really in my wheelhouse."

"Exactly. Would you mind handing me that green bag over there?"

Not paying attention, I nearly jump out of my damn skin when Abi's fingers graze across mine when she hands me my tool bag. I clear my throat quickly and pull the cleaning supplies out from underneath the cabinet. That's when another genius idea hits me. Obviously, Abi isn't comfortable trying to do this herself...so what if I taught her?

12

ABIGAIL

I'm still kind of confused as to why Jamie's over here, replacing a garbage disposal that I only briefly brought up before, but I guess I can't really say no. And why would I? It's true, the apartment manager had plenty of chances to take this darn thing out just so I could have replaced, but he never did, and it was just another thing to add to the growing list of things frustrate me about my apartment. I suppose I should be grateful that I have my space.

"I can actually show you how to do this if you want me to."

It takes me a moment to recognize that Jamie's talking to me, still kind of lost in my own thoughts. "I'm sorry, what was that?"

Jamie sits up from his spot on the floor, giving me a funny look. "I mean if you don't want me to, it's okay. I have no problem handling it on my own, obviously. I just thought maybe you'd like to see how it's done. In case you ever need to fix anything with the disposal, yourself."

I lick my lips. "Oh. You want me to — to help you?" I can't fake the surprise on my face. No one's ever assumed that I could help with something like this in the first place, much less ask me to. Something sweet and fleeting brushes through my chest. "Sure. I mean I don't know what in the world any of this is, or what I can do to help but... yeah, yeah I can do that."

Jamie's smile is too wide for me to look at it anymore, so I bend down and watch as he pulls out some kind of tool...okay, just a screwdriver I guess, from his green bag.

"Okay, so the first step here is to remove the old unit. We're going to start by taking off the drain arm, and then the tube." Loosening one of the screws in place, he sets down the screwdriver and leans in further, a total look of concentration on his face. The way he sort of sticks the tip of his tongue out to the side has me trying not to breathe too hard.

"All right, so I'm going to need my slip-joint pliers, right there in the top of the bag," he says, pointing to a yellow and red pair of pliers, I'm assuming.

I hold them up. "These?"

"Yep, those are the ones. So I'm going to take this and gently disconnect the drain arm from the main disposal unit, and then I'm going to take out the tube. See? Easy as pie."

With a few snips from his tools and a quick tug, the entire old garbage disposal is pulled out at our feet. The foul smell hits both of us at the same time, and Jamie and I both cover up our noses with the collars of our shirts.

"Jesus! It's a damn good thing I'm getting this out of here. Any longer sitting in there, and your kitchen would have smelled like this!"

I lean further away from the smelly piece of junk. "And then you would have found me passed out somewhere on the floor. Ugh."

"Yeah," he nods, "That's definitely gonna need a trash bag."

I listen along and help Jamie every step of the way, paying attention to all the pieces and all the tools he's using. It may not all stay in my brain forever, but that doesn't matter. At least he's taking the time to show me and to fix all of it too.

His knee nudges up against mine more and more, until our entire legs and hips are pushed up against each other, and I'm trying so hard to keep it together. I don't want to shy away from him, push him away like before, and I don't want it to be obvious that this is such a turn on for me, so I have to play it cool. Besides, he didn't come here to get me all hot and bothered. He came here to fix this stupid sink. Two totally different things. He's just trying to be nice, that's all.

Nice and brotherly.

I swallow, feeling guilty. I imagine our parent's faces if they knew the things we've done. If they could hear my thoughts, they'd never speak to me again.

When Jamie finally sits back to inspects our work, he smiles over at me. "Voila! All finished! See, that wasn't hard, was it? You could probably handle something like this next time, right?" He says this with a smile as though he actually believes it and something cold slices through me just for split second. "What is it?" he asks me.

"It's nothing," I quickly say, not wanting to drag Jamie down at my own dark thoughts as well.

But this is Jamie we're talking about, and he's nothing if not relentless. "You know you can talk to me, Abi. About anything."

Warmth spreads through me, filling the cold void that my realization had caused. "It's just that all of this maintenance stuff is something that I'm not used to, and it's not just because I'm a woman or anything, it's just that…well, Cody used to handle this sort of thing. And he never offered…"

"To teach any of it to you?" he finishes for me, sitting back up again. "Big surprise there. I'm more surprised that his dumbass could handle changing a light bulb, much less anything more than that."

It always used to bother me when the twins talked about Cody like this, but now I could hardly care less. They were both absolutely right — Cody was a complete idiot, and the fact that I let him handle any of the house maintenance stuff makes me mad.

When Jamie shifts to the side to get a look at me, I find myself feeling a little overexposed, even though I'm wearing plain around the house clothes. The twins have this crazy effect on me where the moment they look at me right my eyes, I know I can't look anywhere else.

"It's not hard to learn, as you can see, and I'd be happy to teach you if you want. It doesn't just have to be about foul-smelling garbage disposals, either," he says, grinning as I make a face. "I think it's a good thing to want to know how to handle anything that comes your way. I mean of course it's not a substitute for hiring a professional, mind you, but it's good to be able to manage your own pipes."

Of course, this sets me off giggling like some stupid schoolgirl, bringing my hand up to my mouth trying to hide it. Jamie and his ridiculous dirty jokes, I swear.

"You're probably going to have to get some caulk, you're gonna want that on tap so that it's there whenever you're ready for it," he eyes me, leaning in closer with a huge grin on his face, making me laugh even harder. "It definitely wouldn't hurt to grease the pipes yourself though, there are plenty of oil-based lubricants out there."

"Oh my God, Jamie, stop it," I say, wheezing in between the belly laughs. It would be hard to find anyone who makes me laugh as hard as he does, and in a moment of losing my inhibitions, the cute smile he's giving me sends a thrill down my spine. His eyes soften, and he has me absolutely hooked. There's no way I could look anywhere else but directly back at him.

So I close my eyes, but instead of trying to avoid his stare, I only lean in further and bridge the gap between us, feeling my lips on his, already drowning in him, helpless.

His lips are hot below mine, and I feel myself rising up on my knees, my hands tangling around in his hair and just about to —

"Sorry. I have another job I need to get to," he says gently against my mouth, effectively pulling away and leaving me feeling way too many things all at once.

I try and recover, quickly shaking my head. "No, I mean, of course you do. I'm sorry... I just..." I let my voice trail off. Now that Jamie is the one pushing me away, I have to respect it. I can't just play with him and Jared's emotions like this, and I looked down at the floor as Jamie pulls himself up to a stand.

"All right, well there you go. Lesson one, changing a garbage disposal because your shit landlord sucks," Jamie says weakly, clearly trying to return things back to normal.

"Just let me know if you have any more things that come up, anything else needs to be fixed… Yeah. I'll talk to you later, Abi."

I don't bother waiting for a hug or anything else, for that matter, because I know I'd be waiting forever. When Jamie finally leaves the apartment, I lean against my kitchen counter, my head my hands.

How have I messed things up so badly between me and my stepbrothers? Just planting a kiss on one of them isn't fair to either of them, but it's like I can't help myself anymore. Being around them does crazy things to my brain, drunk or not.

It's like the both of them are two sides of the same coin, and I want to pocket that coin, keep it, never letting anyone else have it but me. It's unfair to all three of us, but I'm starting to realize slowly that fairness doesn't matter as much to me these days.

13

JARED

"Thanks, Jared. I appreciate it. I'm not as bendy as I used to be when I was your age," Mr. McCallum laughs, handing me the signed receipt. "Getting old is for the birds."

I clap him on the back. "Nah. Nothing wrong with vintage," I reply. "Anyway, with any luck, the icemaker won't cause you any more problems."

I slide into the work at hand, going over the paperwork from my last job, making sure I didn't miss anything. With my thoughts so cluttered by everything that's been happening lately, I'm worried I will. But no, everything seems to check out, so I throw the van into drive and head home, ready to relax after another long day.

As I turn onto our street I immediately notice Abi's standing on her tiptoes, trying to push a large trash bag into the apartment's dumpster by the curb. That's all it takes for me to pull alongside her, rolling down my window. It's not as if I can avoid her anyway. "Hey there."

Abi lets out a little shriek as the top of the dumpster closes shut loudly, and turns back to me, giving me a little wave. "Hey. Did you just get home from work?"

I nod. "Yeah. Eight jobs today, can you believe it? Luckily most of them were really small things that only took like half an hour if that. What are you up to?"

Abi shields her eyes from the sun and leans into the van. "It's my day off, so I've just been kind of hanging around the house. I was thinking about what I wanted for dinner, but I still don't know."

"How are you holding up? I mean... I haven't really checked in with you about Cody and all...you haven't had any more trouble from friends have you?"

"Cody, who?" There's a small smile that lights up just enough of her face. "Really, though, I'm okay. Just taking it one day at a time."

Pushing my hair out of my face, I smile right back at her. "That-a-girl."

There's a moment of awkward silence between us before she breaks it by asking me, "When was the last time you cut your hair?"

"Uh, I don't really know. Maybe a couple of months ago?"

Abi just snorts, shaking her head at me. "Have you taken a look at the mirror lately? You totally need a haircut. Before you know it, not even I am going to be able to tell the difference between you and Jamie."

Call me crazy, but something about that idea it doesn't really sit well with me.

"Why don't you come inside my apartment? I can give you a haircut. I used to cut my dad's hair all the time before he started going to his favorite barbershop down the street from the house. What do you say?"

I blink, not really sure of what to make of Abi's offer, but I'm not going to turn down a chance to spend time with her. No way in hell. "Sure. I mean as long as it's not imposing on you or anything…"

I start to get out, watching her closely, wishing I was privy to what's going through her mind. Abi rarely, if ever, just invites us over to hang out, much less do anything for us. And it's not that she's not sweet and caring enough to, it's just that she's always kind of kept herself distanced from me and Jamie. At least until now, anyway.

"Well, are you coming?" she asks with a smile.

I follow her back to her apartment, the conversation with Jamie nagging at the back of my mind. This is just a haircut, I tell myself. A haircut just means a haircut, nothing more.

"Okay, so where do you want to do this?" I ask, pretending not to care that Abi blushes furiously at my choice of words."

"Um, stay right here for a minute, I'm just going to bring in a chair from the dining room…" she says, leaving me for a moment to drag in a chair. "Here you go."

She moves for me to sit down and out of nowhere produces a towel to wrap around my shoulders. The moment her fingers graze against the back of my neck I jump. This is going to involve a lot of restraint on my end, I can just feel it.

"Do you usually get your hair wet before you cut it?"

I shake my head. "The guy just cuts it, no hair washing or anything like that."

"All right. Just relax, I promise I won't hurt you," she says, amusement coloring her tone. The sound of scissors snipping away catches me off guard, and I'm wondering if Abi really knows *how* to cut hair. I mean, her dad's hair is always pretty well done, but then again, she did mention something about a barbershop so...I imagine it looking terrible and uneven. How would I explain that to Jamie?

I take a deep breath and say a little internal prayer that Abi has enough scissor skills to make a good job of this. Only time will tell, I guess.

Instead of worrying about my hair, I focus on how close Abi's standing to me. Close enough that I can smell the sweet strawberry shampoo she uses, and feel the warmth of her body when she presses her belly against my shoulder.

Everything about her feels so soft.

And I'm close to getting hard as a result.

Abi steadily snips away at my hair, bits and pieces of it falling away into my lap and on the floor around me. I don't know whether she realizes or not but she starts to hum quietly to herself, something I didn't know she does. It's so damn adorable, that I wish I could comment on it, and maybe ask her what she's humming. But that would probably just make her stop, so I stay quiet and listen with a smile.

I don't expect the way she runs her fingers along my hair, trying to make sure there are no strays left behind, but she's dragging her nails slightly over my scalp, sending insane tingles up and down my spine, until I'm wishing I could take her up on washing my hair. In the shower. Naked. Together.

"You know, I had no idea how thick your hair was," she muses, her voice still softer from the humming. "It's a wonder you don't have to get it cut every few weeks."

Another scalp tingle runs through me and I fight every urge to shiver under her touch. "I've never really noticed."

Abi brings a comb out of nowhere and pulls it through my hair, the humming finishing off with a cheerful, "Voila!"

She hands me a small mirror to check out her handiwork and I turn it this way and that, looking out how evenly she kept everything. Not too much off the sides, and enough off the top that I don't look like some '90s boy band singer.

In the reflection I see a hopeful look on her face, weighing heavier on me than I thought it would. I can see it in her eyes—she's looking for some sort of validation here.

"Very nice," I say casually, genuinely impressed with her skills. "Now what do I owe you?" I hand her the mirror back and sit up straight, smoothing out the top of my hair.

"I'd say that installing a new garbage disposal seems like a pretty fair trade."

"Oh, does it need to be replaced? I wouldn't mind handling that for you, especially since you turned me back into a decent-looking person once again," I smile, eyeing the kitchen sink. "Do you need me to go ahead and do it? I'd have to order the kit, of course, but as soon as—"

The funny look on her face stops me abruptly. "I mean, Jamie already did it."

Now I'm the one confused. "He did?" I frown.

Abi shifts her feet, uncomfortably. "Jamie came by earlier with a new one and replaced it for me. You didn't know?"

I'm pretty sure my eye twitches well past normalcy, but I don't seem to care. Jamie's been over here. And while doing something like replacing a disposal seems pretty innocuous, I know my twin well enough to know his real intentions. Sure, he probably thought he was just being helpful, but that's how Jamie's brain works. Where some guy would give his girl flowers and candy, Jamie unclogs pipes and fixes creaky doors.

"I didn't know," I finally reply, not quite meeting her eyes. I have a feeling that if I do, she'll be able to read me loud and clear. "But it's fine, Abi."

Pure relief washes over her features.

"So...when did he replace it for you? Was it today?"

"Yep," she says, a broom appearing in her hand. "He said he took off early so he could come install it for me. It was really kind of him, I mean I didn't ask for it and he just showed up with the box for it. Turns out it really needed to be taken out."

Intrigued, I nod. "He just came in and fixed it, then left?"

She hesitates for a moment, the sweeping frozen until she starts back up again. "Well, not quite. He came in and then instead of doing it all by himself, he taught me about plumbing."

"I get it," I interrupt, not seeing the point in wasting time wondering what else they may have been working on in here. As amusing as it is to me, Jamie up to something. There was no way this was just about a waste disposal. Which certainly changes things with us in her apartment right now.

She takes a step back as I stand up, looking somewhat sheepish, but something changes in her eyes. "Hey, did you want me to maybe wash your hair for you? I see a whole bunch of little bits of hair around your neck and all."

"Sure," I say, wondering what Abi's game is. I walk over to the sink.

"Okay, let me just grab the shampoo from my bathroom…"

The moment I smell the delicious scent of strawberries my knees nearly buckle. It's the scent I most closely associate with her, and once her hands are running through my hair to wet it, I feel myself getting way too excited about a simple shampooing. It doesn't help that I'm slammed up against the damn kitchen cabinets.

She's humming again, her voice even sweeter this time around. "Keep your eyes closed," she whispers next to my ear, and my cock thickens.

I do as I'm told, but it only makes it easier to think about what she's doing and how she's probably leaning far over, her tank-top pulled away from her chest. If I was facing in that direction, I'd get a nice view of her pretty tits.

Just like that, it's over too quickly, and Abi quickly runs the towel over my head, drying off my hair.

My brain has been put on temporary hiatus when she pushes my shoulder to lean back, and I find myself staring up at her gorgeous face, my eyes unable to stop from trailing down to her chest and stomach, where splotches of wet water stains cling to her.

I stand up slowly, my eyes moving back up to her lips, seeing the way they're slightly parted. She's only inches away, and the gap seems to be closing by the second.

I'm kissing Abi again, and this time it's just me and her in the empty, private space of her apartment. My hands are gathered up in her hair, and I'm backing her up against the counter, her hands tangled up in my shirt, pulling me even closer.

When she gasps against my lips it just drives me deeper into this forbidden territory, and I'm tasting her jaw, her neck, kissing back up to her ear, trailing my tongue back to her lips where I kiss her harder, more desperate this time. My mind is going a million miles an hour and I'm sure I'm going to lose this moment if I don't run with it, if we don't—

With one hand, she pushes gently away from me, disentangling our bodies until we're far enough away from each other that we can look at each other properly. "I'm sorry, Jared. I…I don't know if this is such a good idea."

Rebuffed again and my mind teetering on the edge of some crazy precipice, I'm starting to really not like this feeling. I have to adjust myself by twisting to the side, hoping she doesn't notice the strain against my pants that feels like it's a new normal. "Okay, no problem. No pressure."

I see the lump rising in her throat as she sighs. "I don't know what we're doing," she says.

"What do you mean?"

"I…I kissed Jamie too when he was here…and now this…" she glances at the floor and my heart pounds. She kissed Jamie too?

"We have to stop…all of us," she says.

14

JAMIE

I don't remember what it's like not knowing how to cook. Ever since we were little, Mom made sure Jared and I knew the basics. By the time we were ten we knew how to cook chili, grilled cheese sandwiches, hot dogs, and even make a homemade pizza. I've always been proud of that, but looking down at the half-ass spaghetti and meatballs isn't really giving me that vibe.

Outside of the kitchen, I hear Jared come in, his boots hitting the floor a little heavier than normal. "Hey, in here. Hope spaghetti's okay. The noodles are kind of overcooked and mushy, but I'm sure it's all right…"

Jared's standing at the entryway to the kitchen, glaring. "You're in a very charitable mood today."

Confused, I look back down at the pitiful noodles in the pot. "I always cook us dinner."

Jared smirks. "No, Jamie. I'm not talking about dinner. I thought we agreed not to go after Abigail?"

"What?"

"The waste disposal. You just happened to be passing with an expensive bit of hardware, I suppose."

"I found the one you lost before, and I knew Abi needed one. No big deal."

Jared steps further into the kitchen, leaning up against the refrigerator. "And feeling her up wasn't part of the plan?"

Forgetting about the noodles, I take a step closer too. "No, no. It wasn't like that. All I did was just…wait, how do you know about that?"

Now that I'm closer to my brother, something stands out like a sore thumb. Mom recently mentioned something about Jared needing a haircut, and funny enough, it seems his hair is magically shorter since I saw him this morning. For someone with a supposed eight or nine calls today, he sure had enough time to go to the barber. "Nice haircut," I add. "Dude, you were just there, too, weren't you?"

Jared waves me away, but I'm not letting him off that easily, especially as he's acting all pissy about me helping Abi. "No, you were. That's how you know about the garbage disposal. So, you came home to chew me out, but you did the same fucking thing! Go figure, asshole! What else happened? Did she give you a nice trim? Maybe rub your shoulders a little bit? Maybe rub something else, too?"

Jared grits his teeth at me but looks away, and that's when I know I got him. "You know I'll be honest. We kissed. It happened. We stopped though."

As if that's any consolation. "Nice."

He's back to the pissed off expression he walked in with. "So you're telling me nothing like that happened when you went over there earlier?"

"I didn't say that. Abi, she...kissed me. But I broke it off because we already agreed."

The timer on the stove goes off, breaking us both of the tension between us. I flip off the dial for the sauce and turn back to my brother. "What a right fucking pair we are."

Jared pulls away from the refrigerator, shrugging. "I think we have to face the facts, Jamie. It's clear we both feel something for her. And as much as she's fighting it, she seems to like us too. The question is, what do we do about it?"

I lean against the wall across from him and sigh, unsure of how to really answer him. "I don't know, man. If it were easy, we wouldn't be having a mother's meeting about it."

And it's true. We've shared some wild ass chicks in the past, and there was always this unspoken agreement where we never really did much else with them past a one-night stand type deal. But this is Abi and not only do we have to think about her feelings in this situation, but there's always the chance that this could cause a much bigger problem with our family. And there's no way we want any part of that.

"Did she kiss you?" I finally ask the question that's been burning in my head that past few minutes finally bursting through.

Jared shuffles his feet until they leave a small scuff mark on the linoleum. "I kissed her."

I don't know whether to be angry with him or to gloat. "And you come in here to make me feel guilty."

"I don't know how you stopped it. It was damn near impossible for me, and I'm the one who initiated things with her."

But that's the thing with Abi. She makes you feel like that the only option is whatever gets you closest to her.

15

ABIGAIL

"Toast or eggs?" I look around at my empty apartment and solemnly swear to invest in a furry creature to talk to so that I don't look like a crazy person mumbling to myself so much.

I break out the egg carton, but for some reason, the idea of a tomato and mushroom omelet isn't as appetizing as it used to be. I shove them back into the refrigerator, and instead, stick a couple of pieces of bread into the toaster, but even the toast smothered in the usual strawberry jam doesn't really do it for me. I frown at the half-eaten food on my plate hating the prospect of wasting food it, but my stomach is starting to rebel at the idea of eating so early.

Since I'm running a little behind this morning—I must have been super exhausted from yesterday's morning's shift—I don't have time to make much else and scramble to put on my work clothes. Work. Just what I need to keep me from thinking about both Jared and Jamie's lips on mine this week.

"You look a little peaky. Are you okay?" Dandie says as I slip my apron over my head.

"Yep. Everything's good," I answer, giving her a smile. Dandie is one of the sweetest people I've ever known, but she's always worrying over the littlest things with me and Shay.

Speaking of Shay… "Shay's due in around 12:30, right?"

Dandie nods, pushing her reading glasses back up her nose. "Yes, ma'am. You're free to go after two."

--

It takes some working, but I manage to clear out all the work orders from the night before, plus the two that came in while Dandie was running the cash register in the front. It's been a nice distraction, but my stomach isn't too happy with having to heave this way and that any time I have to bend over for something. Hopefully, I'm not catching the stomach flu.

"Hallelujah, it's raining food!" Shay sings at the top of her lungs, spinning around with a large brown paper bag in her hand as she comes in through the back door. "Lunch is on the house, my friend. I managed to sweet-talk the owner next door into throwing in a few free egg rolls."

I'm totally famished but after the way my stomach was acting earlier, I'm not really sure I'm ready to dive into lunch just yet. It's from my absolute favorite sushi place so I'd be crazy to say no.

Shay opens the bag of food and I swear I nearly keel right over.

The smell. Oh god, the smell! My stomach lurches as the scent of fresh sushi and greasy fried egg rolls waft past my nose, completely overwhelming the sweeter, subtler scent of the shop. "Oh no," I moan, grabbing my stomach. "I don't think I should eat anything."

Shay gives me a funny look. "What? I thought you'd be starving by now. Did you order lunch earlier, or something?"

I shake my head, the tension in my stomach fading off a bit.

Seemingly not paying much attention, Shay sits the bag on the little wooden table in the middle of the room, cracking open one of the Styrofoam containers. "You finished up the last of the advance orders, right? I know there were like three or four of them when I got in yesterday," she says, putting the food down and pulling the latest order ticket off the clipboard Dandie keeps hung up above the ribbons. "But no customers, so it wasn't a big deal."

My stomach roils again, and I'm trying to decide if I need to make a run for the bathroom or not. "Well, we'll see how it goes today," I reply through the grimace that won't wear off.

"You okay, girl? You look like you've just smelled the world's sweatiest ball-sack."

"Not. Helping. Shay."

Chuckling, she finishes depositing the money into our cash bag. "Sorry, couldn't resist. But really though, you don't look too good. Did you eat something off today?"

The very last thing I want to talk about is food at the moment. "I think it's the sushi," I mumble, trying so hard to concentrate. "And I did do up the last advanced order today. There were only two so far."

The look Shay gives me is unmistakable and the possible reason for my tummy woes hits me like a ton of bricks. "Your favorite California spring rolls are making you feel sick?"

Even though my mouth is now as dry as cotton, panic surging through me like molten metal, I wipe my hands on my apron and shrug. Morning sickness. Ugh. I shake my head as though that's gonna work to remove the shudder-inducing realization. "Well, I mean maybe they're just not cooked well enough. They have a new chef in there, and I noticed last time that the burger was a little extra greasy, so maybe that's why it's making me feel gross." It's the lamest response in the long history of me and Shay's friendship, so I'm not at all surprised when she doesn't buy it.

"God, when I was pregnant with Kevin? Ugh. I remember I couldn't eat Thai food for the whole nine months and I even waited after that until I was absolutely positive it wouldn't make me sick anymore. It was that bad. Imagine…no red curry for over nine months! I swear I'm not having any more kids…"

Shay cuts the next strip of ribbon, obviously waiting for me to chime in, but when I don't, she turns slowly to look at me. "But that was just me, and this is probably just some stomach bug or something, probably. Right?"

Almost instinctively, I fight the urge to touch my stomach, even though I know I won't find anything there yet. All the blood drains from my face. In fact, it feels like all the everything in my body has just drained away, leaving me as a sad sack of skin on the floor. I take a deep breath, trying to remain calm. But all I can think is, fuck…fuck…fuck…

"You're not pregnant?" Her voice isn't as strong as it usually is.

Shay's hand slips from its usual place on her hip, and she reaches out to touch my shoulder, concern plain as day on her face. "I mean, it's not possible, right?" She lowers her voice, checking to make sure Dandie and the customer up front can't hear us. "You and Cody were...being all weird and chaste, right? Didn't you tell me something about Cody wanting to wait until the actual wedding to have sex again?" There's a pause and then, "Fuck, girl. Do we need to go get you a pregnancy test?"

The only thing that is making any sense in the world right now is snipping the ends off the stems of the cascade's flowers—because things like pregnancy tests just don't compute.

It wouldn't be Cody's baby. It couldn't be Cody's baby...because Shay's right. Cody had been acting weird for a couple of months leading up to the engagement party. He kept pushing off sex with me, claiming it would make it even 'hotter' if we held back as much as we could until the actual wedding. I wasn't a fan of the idea at all, but there really wasn't much of a choice given to me.

I crunch the numbers in my head. I've had my period since he mentioned that, twice, in fact. My stomach fills with lead, practically bringing me to my knees right here in the middle of the shop.

If there's a baby, it can't be Cody's baby.

It would be Jamie's. Or Jared's. And there's no way of telling which one...

"We need to go. I need to get out of here right now," I say desperately, clinging to the edge of the counter. "Where's the closest place I can find a pregnancy test?"

16

JARED

"We need to figure this out." Jamie steps into the mudroom, throwing his tool bag onto the bench. "I couldn't concentrate worth shit today. And I'm fucking tired of it."

"I know," I reply, sighing. "I'm the same."

I can tell just by looking at my brother's face that he's frustrated and I get it.

"So, what are we going to do, then?"

Heading into the living room, I drop down onto the couch and rub my temples. It's been a long day with Abi and my feelings for her on my mind.

"Look at you. You look like shit!" Jamie exclaims. "We need to figure out what to do. Like, right now."

He's not wrong. When Abi was just an impossible fantasy, I could push her to the back of my mind. I could pretend to myself that I was okay with how things were, but now I'm not. I know what it's like to wrap her copper hair around my fingers and feel her soft, pale thighs around me. I know how it feels to have her fingers run through my hair. All of these torturous thoughts are circling around and around in my head, followed by the pang of jealousy that threads through them. Jamie and Abi on their own, laughing, kissing, holding each other. It's like some kind of macabre merry-go-round. Whatever the case may be, we have to establish that there is no separating us, at the very least. There is no way I could deal with being the third wheel.

"Yeah, okay." I stand up a few feet away from Jamie and pull out my phone.

"Okay... What?"

"We need to settle this now. No more skirting around it. I'm tired, you're tired, and if we don't go over there and tell Abigail what the deal is, it's just going to keep going on like this. I don't know about you, but that doesn't exactly sound like a walk in the park to me."

He nods. "All right. Good. We got a game plan going now. So we go over there and say what exactly."

He brings up a good point.

"Ah, well, yeah. We should probably figure that out." I scratch at the five o'clock shadow that I didn't have the energy to shave off this morning.

"We both want her, right?" he asks.

"I think that's the consensus here, yeah."

Jamie shrugs. "Then we tell her we get to share. That's the only way things can work with us."

"We get to share? I don't know, Jamie, I don't want Abi thinking she's just some kind of object to us. Like we're fighting over a toy or something."

He frowns, his eyebrows drawing closer. "Well, what do we tell her, then? She needs to know the score…"

Holding up my hand, I cut him off. "Yeah, I know, man. But it's the way we phrase it, you know what I mean? It's not us sharing her, it's her sharing us. I don't want us to come off like some a barbarian, that's all. I don't think that would go over well with her."

"All right, fine, but we do need her to be clear on that bit. She has to know that this is a combined thing, here. Both of us, or neither of us. I want her to know that we both feel the same for her, too."

It would be easy to think of anyone else's feelings for Abi as less than mine, but the way Jamie's eyes blaze under his furrowed brow is enough to remind me that's not the case with him, my twin brother. "Right," I agree, leaning up against the threshold of the doorway. "Now we just need to wait to for her to get home."

Jamie casually peeks through the blinds, before looking over his shoulder back at me. "That should be no problem. She's walking up the sidewalk to her apartment right now."

"Let's wait for a few minutes. Let her get sorted."

"Yeah. Okay."

We both sit on the sofa and stare at the TV which currently isn't on. I turn to my brother and he's biting his fingernails as though he's nervous. My brother isn't usually bothered by this kind of thing. He's a take-it-leave-it kind of guy, I guess because there is never a shortage of women who are interested. With Abi, though, he's different. He's not his usual cocky self.

"Stop looking at me like that," he mumbles under his breath just loud enough for me to hear him.

"What?"

"You know what."

"I have no idea what you're talking about."

He shoots me his trademark pissed off look. "You're looking at me like you're wondering why the hell I'm so bothered about all this."

I shrug, used to Jamie's ability to read my mind. It's a twin thing, I guess.

"Abi's special," he says sternly. "She's always been different. Maybe it's because I've had the chance to get to know her for so long. I don't know. All I know is that if she says no, I don't know what the fuck I'm gonna do about it. I don't think I can stand by and let her start dating another one of these fuckwits who has no idea what an amazing girl she is or how to treat her. I don't want to just be her stepbrother anymore."

I nod. "It's how I feel too."

"That's good then, isn't it? We both feel the same way. No jealousy. No divisiveness. This is what I want."

I grin at my brother. "Guess we'd better get over there and convince that woman to be our girl."

We make our way over to Abi's apartment. The warmth of the sun is perfect against my skin. As I stroll beside my brother, a sense of 'rightness' settles over me. There are days when I think that Jamie has the capacity to drive me insane, but I don't know what I'd do if one of us found a girl and wanted to move on without the other. I've never been without him. Not even for a day. I know it's clichéd to say but he's like my other half. If we can convince Abi that we want her, and not just for a fling, maybe this is the answer. I'll have to share the woman I want but that means that I get to keep my brother close too. It seems like the ideal solution.

There's only one problem.

Abi.

She's been so resistant. The thing is we haven't told her how we feel. Not really. I guess this is make or break.

Abi makes next to no noise though, when she slowly pulls the door open, her eyes fixated on a spot somewhere between me and my brother. Something feels off the moment she shifts away from us to let us inside, still not quite meeting our eyes. It dawns on me that she may be feeling something too, especially having kissed both me and Jamie in the same twenty-four hours, but I keep it to myself as we head inside after her.

"Hey, Abi." Jamie breaks the silence.

"Hi," she replies softly, fidgeting with the lace on her shirt. If I didn't know any better, I would think she looked like she might cry. This is not good.

"Abigail... Abi. We wanted to come over and talk to you about what's been going on –"

"Between the three of us," Jamie adds.

It's here where I notice how flushed her cheeks are, but I don't want my concern for her to get in the way of the conversation. "Yes, we need to talk about that. Me and Jamie have been talking about it, and we have to be truthful with you. This whole going back and forth between being with us, and then not wanting to be with us, but then more kissing and uh," I clear my throat, "and things like that...we can't keep doing this."

"And it's not that we don't want to do the kissing and the things like that," Jamie adds his eyes darting to mine for a second, sending what I imagine to be violent death threats via his mind. "But we need to know where we stand...and where you stand."

"We both have feelings for you, but I think you already know that...and we're not willing to let our feelings for you come in between us," I explain taking another step closer to Abi. "The only way this could work is if you are willing to be with both of us."

Jamie steps closer to her, his gaze intense. "We are a package deal, simple as that and we don't want you to feel like you have to choose between us. You have both of us, however you'd like us. It probably sounds complicated, but it's —"

Abi shakes her head, some kind of panic coloring her features. "No, it's not that. I just... Well, I don't know who..." her voice trails off, and I take the opening, suddenly remembering the guilty look she had when she first answered the door.

"Abi, you don't have to feel bad about kissing both of us. There's no need to feel guilty. We could make it work, I promise you," I say as her eyes widen. Taking her clammy hand in mine.

She stares down at our hands and then slips hers out of mine, turning to pick up a small glass of water behind me. I don't do anything but watch as she slowly drains the glass.

"I have something I need to tell you," she stutters, chewing on her bottom lip like crazy. All I want to do is to soothe it, run my tongue along it and hold her in my arms again. I don't understand why she looks like she's about to run away.

"What? What's wrong?" Jamie asks, closing up the space between the three of us.

She takes a deep breath and says something that blows my fucking mind.

"I'm pregnant."

17

JAMIE

I'm completely frozen, probably stuck in this position with my jaw unhinged, looking like a goddamn cartoon character, forever.

Pregnant.

Shit. With Cody's baby? What the hell is she going to do now?

Abi squints up at us, waiting.

Waiting for a response. What can I say? Congratulations? Like fuck I can.

This is the woman I want to be mine.

There's barely any space between me and Abi and Jared, but it feels like we all just got put on one of those carnival rides where the floor drops away from your feet because you're spinning so fast. I don't get how everything is standing so still, so silent, but my insides feel like I'm in a blender.

Jared comes to his senses first. "Do you…" He clears his throat and tries again. Do you know who the father is?"

I haul off and punch him right in his damn arm. What the fuck is his problem? "What the hell, man? You can't just go around asking people who knocked them up!"

Abi sticks up for him, holding her hands up and stepping in between us. It's okay, Jamie. It's a totally valid question. And I get why you're asking," she says quickly. "This is so difficult to tell you."

Jared puts his hand on Abi's shoulder. "It's okay. Just take your time."

"It's can't be Cody," she says softly. "We didn't do anything…you know…sexually in a few months."

I stare at her. Not Cody's. That's good. But who's is it? A flash of the night we all had sex crosses my mind. The feeling of pushing inside her. It was so fucking good…I wasn't wearing a rubber.

Fuck.

Abi shifts from foot to foot, looking a little green. Is she feeling sick? Sick from the pregnancy or sick from having to tell us. "I don't know…who the father is?"

For the second time, my stomach seems to drop. Could it be someone else's? Maybe Jared and I weren't the only men she's been drowning her sorrows in. The thought makes me want to punch the fucking wall.

"What do you mean?" Jared says quietly.

"I mean…neither of you wore a condom, did you? That means it could be either of you."

It takes a few seconds for her words to sink in. Seems I wasn't the only reckless fucker that night. "You didn't wear a condom?" I turn to Jared. He shakes his head looking sheepish. We're usually meticulous about using contraception. Neither of us wanted to have any kids and not be around for them full time. We had that enough when we were growing up.

There's this weird quiet moment where I'm looking at Jared, Jared looking at me.

He shakes his head and I think his expression must be a mirror image of mine. We've fucked up. I can't imagine how Abi must be feeling right now.

"I'm sorry," I say to her. "We should have been more careful."

Abi shakes her head. "I was there too. I could have told you."

"We were all lost in the moment," Jared says gently.

I take in a breath to give myself a moment to gather my thoughts. I'm not usually good at dealing with 'feelings'. They're too subtle for me to wrap my head around, but I get that she must be feeling worried right now. "What are you thinking, Abi? How do you feel about it?"

She gazes up at me, her eyes glassy and my heart fucking shatters. I don't want her to cry. Not now. Not ever.

"I don't know," she says. "Shocked. I mean, I was supposed to be getting engaged and now that's over and this…" She puts her hand protectively over her stomach and I get a fucking lump in my throat. "I have a life inside of me, and I didn't think it would ever happen this way…you know…without planning it."

Jared nods. "Do you need anything? Is there anything we can do for you?"

"Whatever you need, Abi," I agree.

The look of nervousness on Abi's face fades into something less panicky "I don't know what I need right now...other than time...and space. I just can't get my mind to wrap around what's happening...and I need to think things through." She pauses. "But I appreciate you guys worrying about me. I'm trying to keep it all straight in my head, you know?"

The way she says it doesn't sound ominous but it still doesn't stop the way my stomach twists in on itself. What exactly does she need time to think about?

"We can give you that," Jared replies, stepping aside and giving her some actual space. Wait, we can?

I find myself nodding and doing the same, despite the way everything in me is screaming to tell her that I want her and I want this baby. "Yeah, whatever you need, Abi," is what my mouth actually says.

Abi bites down softly on her bottom lip. "Thank you. I'm so tired right now. It's so early but it's really affecting me. I think I'm going to make myself something quick to eat and call it a night. I'll call you guys when I know...when I work things out, okay?"

What she's saying is so vague. How can we walk away like this? Abi's not herself and with all the shit that she's been through over the past few months, I don't want to leave her to deal with this by herself.

We're back to not knowing. We're no further forward but what can we do? I turned to Jared, desperate for his usual relaxed way with the words.

"Yes, it's definitely been a long day. For all of us. Just let us know whenever you're ready to talk again."

I'm the first to go in for a hug, but it's awkward — somehow being too intimate and not intimate enough for me — so I end up giving her a quick squeeze and pat on her back. The smell of her sweet shampoo tickles my nose, making me want to pull her closer back to me, but she's already stepped out of range and Jared gives her a pretty weird-looking hug as well, the strange look on his face giving him away. He hates the idea of waiting just as much as I do.

By the time we're out the door again, my chest feels tighter than ever before. Once we make it to the sidewalk that leads up to her apartment building, I stop, needing to get it out. "What the hell are we going to do, Jared?"

18

ABIGAIL

I've already lost count of how many times I've had to go to the bathroom, so when Jamie shows up on my doorstep with his arms full of groceries to stock up my apartment, I'm pretty sure my heart melts into a puddle. One less thing for me to have to deal with even though the thought of food right now makes me want to chuck up everything inside me.

"You so did not have to do all this," I say, trying to keep it together long enough to thank him for all the help. "It's just this whole morning sickness thing. I sorta always thought it was something that most women just played up, but no way. It's here and it is real," I sigh. "So, really, thank you. I don't think I'm able to go very far on my own without some kind of barf bag."

He makes a face as he starts unloading the items. "It's fine. I feel for you. I fucking hate being sick to my stomach, almost as much as Jared."

I lift a brow at him, opening the refrigerator to put away the milk. "Oh yeah?"

"Yep. If Jared even thinks he has a stomachache coming on he'll start flipping out, getting all sweaty and weird. It's kind of funny, actually."

The corner of his mouth quirks up, and I know that he loves revealing less than admirable traits about his brother, in an effort to level the so-called 'playing field.' But in reality, they're as equal to me as can be.

So equal in fact, that barely an hour passes before I get a text from Jared, asking me if I have a massage parlor preference.

"A what?" I ask as soon as I hear his calm 'Hi, Abi,' on the phone. "I don't really have a massage parlor. I've gone literally once, and it was because my dad gave me a discount code for a hot stone massage, like, three years ago."

"Are you familiar with Serenity Holistic Spa Center? I've read plenty of good reviews about it. They have a specific masseuse who handles all the prenatal massages there. You're off on Thursday and Saturday this week, right?" I can hear him flipping through pages of paper, the scratching of his pencil near the phone.

"Well, yeah, but...wait. Aren't prenatal massages for women who are very obviously pregnant and have to be careful with traditional massages?" So what, I read a book or three about pregnancy in the past week...?

Jared's quiet for a moment. "If that's true, that's okay. At least you'll have plenty of practice sessions. I think if we book multiple appointments we can get you a pretty good discount..."

And that's just the beginning between the two of my boys.

One day Jamie's getting me way too many groceries and Jared's booking way too many massage appointments...the next, they're both over at my apartment, the sound of various hammering going on.

"This window needs to have the screen replaced. What if the baby climbs up and pushes through it? They'll fall out!" Jared calls out, his hands already prying the screen from its spot on the window sill's track.

"But Jared...I live on the first floor," I reply, watching him and shaking my head.

At the other end of the house, Jamie's fixing a closet door that gets stuck when you try to shut it.

"It won't take too much more than some good ol' WD-40, and some re-adjusting the door hinge brackets. No big deal." The busy sound of his electric drill and the stench of WD-40 oil hits me right in the stomach, and I barely have a chance to say much else before I'm running to the bathroom, glad that he seems to have it together.

On and on it goes all week, until I have to beg them not to try and do something ridiculous like reupholstering my furniture. I'm not even all that surprised when Jared stares longingly at the dark brown sofa.

"But a lighter color would show less baby spit-up..."

I nearly leap for joy when I see Shay's pretty face gracing my doorway. After dealing with the twins all week, I'm definitely ready for some girl time.

"It's still weird," Shay admits, looking me up and down as she tosses her purse over the chair. "I keep forgetting that you're pregnant."

I bite my lip, suddenly feeling a little insecure. "But...I mean, it's not like...bad, or—"

"Oh, no, girl. It's not that at all!" She takes my hands in hers, smiling at me gently. "You know I'll be here for you through everything, whether you do decide to you know...go through with the pregnancy, or not."

I'm a little shocked—shocked enough that my hands drop out of hers. "What? Of course, I'm going through with it, Shay!"

She nods slowly, something very obviously on her mind.

"What? What is it?" My heart starts to race uncontrollably. I don't want my best friend thinking that I'm making a mistake. It's hard enough trying to keep my own worries in check.

"I got you, but you know...you'd do well to have a real serious talk with the, uh...two possible fathers. Make sure you're all on the same page, you know?"

I know Shay's heart is in the right place, and even though I'm still debating if I'm even ready for that talk, deep down, I know she's right.

--

It takes me a full five minutes to finally work up the nerve to text Jared and Jamie and invite them over. It takes less than five minutes though, before they're walking through my door, both clearly on the edges of their seats. I can feel their nervousness even on the other side of the room.

"I've asked you to come over because I think I'm ready to talk about this..." my voice trails off. The corner of my t-shirt crumples in my hands as I twist it, and I take in a good, deep breath. "I don't know how you feel, but to be honest, it won't make any difference. I'm keeping the baby...I can't do anything different, to be honest. I know I can't expect either of you to do anything in this situation…I mean, I don't even know which of you is the father but…I would really appreciate your support if you're willing to offer it."

Jamie nearly jumps up from his spot on the sofa. "Of course we want to help!"

"It should go without saying, Jared adds softly. "Whatever you need, Abi."

It's like having this huge stone lifted right off my chest. I didn't realize I needed to hear them say this so badly. The pit of my stomach loosens up, and I release the breath I'm holding. "Good. Great." I smile. "I'm glad we're all going to figure out this thing together."

In an instant, Jared and Jamie are on either side of me, looking so hopeful that it sends a sharp pang right through my chest. The grins on their faces warm my heart and tears spring to my eyes. I've been trying to be brave but in truth, I'm so damn scared about everything that going to happen next. Growing this baby. Bringing it into the world. Raising it and facing the shock and disapproval of the whole town. Potentially being disowned by my father and stepmother when they find out…

"Oh god," I gasp. "What am I going to tell people?"

"We've got a while to work that out, Abi." Jared says. "You need to focus on keeping yourself healthy and strong and growing this baby the best you can. Don't worry about anything else."

"We'll be the best goddamn dads a kid's ever had, you better believe it," Jamie laughs and I can't help but smile. Over the past week, I've imagined all sorts; raising this child by myself, raising this child with one of the twins, raising it with both. Whichever way I looked at the situation, I couldn't find an option that made me truly happy. On my own, I'd struggle to cope. Single parents just have it so tough and I don't think I'm strong enough to do the kind of job that Natalie, the twins mom, did. Being with just one of my stepbrothers would mean I'd always feel that something was missing. Being with both of them would leave us all potentially scorned and ostracized. Jamie's excitement is so sweet but I just don't have it in me to feel that way yet.

I settle back on the cushion, needing to stretch out my stomach before I risk heaving again. For the briefest moment, I imagine Jamie and Jared taking turns holding a flailing bundle wrapped in a warm baby blanket, tiny toes sticking out at one end, tiny red tufts of hair crowning a small head at the other. My dad always said that any kid of mine would absolutely have to have my carrot-top.

And just like that, the dream burns off into ashes in my mouth. Dad.

"What will our parent's say," I say softly, still trying to shake the taste from my mouth.

This wipes the smiles right off their faces, and for good reason, too. My dad isn't just some guy who wants the best for his little girl, and so on. He's what plenty of people have described as a 'hard-ass.' In fact, I had to physically go over to the house and order him not to go after Cody once he found out that Cody really did dump me on the night of our engagement party. I'd never seen so many veins threatening to burst from someone's forehead before.

Jared and Jamie look even more worried, probably imagining the same thing I am.

"It might be beneficial for us to keep all this quiet. At least for now," Jared suggests as Jamie grinds his jaws together.

It'll be hard to do for sure, but maybe it won't be so difficult with the two of them on my side. I consider my feelings for them together. I stop pushing back at the same conclusion I've had, ever since our first night together, and I let my feelings run free inside my mind, finally.

The truth is that I truly do care for them, even without the whole baby situation going on, but I don't want to have to choose between them and I definitely don't want to cause any friction between either. "We could co-parent, right? That's a thing people do when they're in somewhat similar situations. I've been reading about it in one of the books I picked up." I hate hearing how tiny my voice sounds. So hopeful, like I'm teetering on the edge of a huge cliff and trying not to fall. Jamie tilts his head to the side, considering me slowly. "But why would we have to do that?"

"What Jamie means is that we don't have to necessarily go the co-parenting route." Jared quickly adds, looking back over my head at his brother. "We've already told you...we both have feelings for you, Abi. All we want is for you to be happy, and of course, for the baby to be healthy and safe. You both need us, honey. I know it's unconventional, but what does that matter, really? Families aren't just mom and pop and two kids anymore."

Jared makes it sound so easy. I look between them and I believe they are ready to make the most of our situation, and willing to be with me, really be with me through all of it. But none of their hopefulness will make any difference when it comes to Dad and Natalie. This news is going to be like a bomb exploding, and if I was the subject of gossip because of what happened with Cody, imagine what people will say about me now. My cheeks flush with the imagined shame.

The tears quickly slip down my face before I have a chance to wipe at them as these overwhelming emotions I've been holding in overtake me in one go. I feel so torn between the relief that bubbles inside me and the dread. Jamie pulls me against his broad chest stroking my tears away. Jared kneels in front of me, stroking my legs in comfort.

"It's okay, we can figure this out, Abi. You don't have to cry." Jamie's fingers brush my cheek. His face is so close to mine I can feel the warmth of his breath gust over my skin. He feels big and strong and good; all the things I need to make me feel safe in this time of uncertainty. I don't think either of us intends for our lips to meet the way they do. This is what got us all into this situation. Irrational behavior. Putting our desires before our common sense. I know this but it doesn't stop how my heart craves to feel their closeness. It doesn't stop my need for their strength to surround me.

I reach for Jared's hand and tug him so that he's back on the sofa behind me. His lips kiss my neck so gently I shiver, as Jamie's mouth softly nibbles until I'm almost boneless with the sensation.

I need them.

I need them so much more than I let myself feel at first, and it's all crushing me under its weight.

I bury my hands in Jamie's hair, not caring how messy and wet my face is from the crying, and when I've kissed him enough that he knows exactly how I'm feeling, I turn and do the same to Jared.

"It's okay," Jamie says softly. "We've got you, baby."

It takes time for them to touch me. Time for them to feel that I want it and that they're not overstepping. It's crazy that we're all so tentative after the night that made the baby who's nestling in my womb. When they do, it's as though my body comes to life. The sickness is gone, replaced with a hunger for my stepbrothers that scares me. Cody taught me that it's foolish to rely on anyone and now I'm expecting two men to stand by me through such a tough situation.

"You're so beautiful, Abi," Jared whispers gruffly. My fingers have messed his hair and his eyes look sleepy with desire. He brings me back with his words and all I can do is push aside my fears to be in the moment. No matter what I do now, there's no changing anything that has come before.

These are the days to enjoy while we still can. To be free to be with each other without the judgment of the outside world. I want to feel that way with them while I can for as long as we have.

Someone's fingers fumble for the hem of my shirt, working their hand across my ribs and over the thing fabric of my bra and I don't say no. It's so much to be pressed between them, their mouths hot and needy on my skin.

I let the tears flow, tired of holding back any longer, and my boys don't seem to mind as Jared carries me into my bedroom, laying me down a little too carefully for my taste.

"I'm not going to break," I whisper, raking my nails over his broad, muscular back. "Don't treat me as though I'm fragile."

A baby will change a lot, but this was ours before we even knew.

I take another shaky breath as Jared removes my panties and presses his mouth between my legs. Jamie's mouth kisses my neck over and over, his hands finding my breasts, caressing them gently.

They please me until I can't take anymore. Until I'm lost in a haze of hopes and dreams.

This could be the way it always is. I could love them and they could love me. Our baby would be lucky to have three hearts to own.

I climb higher, nearing an orgasm that feels as though it will break me open, but when it comes it they hold me rooted in the present.

Beautiful, they say. Perfect.

Words that fill me and make me whole.

They listen, they pay attention, and understand what I need. I cling on tightly to both of them, forgetting the worry that has consumed my mind, ignoring the tiny voice telling me to be prepared for the consequences.

I don't listen to it tonight.

I can't.

19

JARED

Abi's sleeping, her hair a tangled coppery mess on the pillow.

I meet Jamie's gaze, the unspoken agreement to slip out of bed and talk about what just went down, already in the air.

Tossing a towel to him, I pull another one around my own waist and follow him into the small living room, hopefully out of earshot from Abi. The floor creaks like a warning to us, and we both freeze, listening to make sure she's still breathing softly and evenly before we sit down.

This isn't like the last time, where my adrenaline was steadily pumping, pushing me for more of Abi, for another shot of her straight to the heart. This is different. Man, when they say babies change everything, they really mean it.

Jamie settles back further into the couch and crosses his arms—his defensive move. It's like he's trying to brace himself for whatever else is about to happen.

"So that just happened. Again."

The clock on the wall loudly ticks the seconds as I think of what to say. "There goes taking everything slow, I guess." It was something Jamie and I have brought up here and there over the past week...ever since Abi told us she was pregnant. We didn't want to overwhelm her with our feelings, especially since we had no idea what she planned on doing. Taking it slow and easy with her was supposed to be the first step in making this all work. At least, that was the original idea. But now? Looking at the space that separates me and my brother, I know the truth. We're in it. For life. Taking it slow or not, it won't matter to us.

But that's if everything else lines up just right, too. Including Abi's actions and words. "Can we really do this, though?" I whisper hoarsely, not at all surprised by the way my throat tightens up around the thought. "We're talking next-level kind of stuff, here, Jamie. This isn't just sharing some random wild drunken night with a girl, and then leaving the next morning. The sex is one thing, sure, but this is serious. This goes beyond just the night. It spans from now until forever. This is making a family work, no matter what."

At least Jamie considers my words for more than a nano-second before shaking his head. "Look, I get it, Jared. We already know all that. And if we ever wanted to have this…this whole family thing on our own...I don't know, man. We've gotta face the facts, here. Anytime one of us is dating someone, it always creates a big problem. It's irritating as hell when someone pulls us apart because you and I both know we've always been too close and too jealous. Remember when you were dating Andrea a few years ago? She complained that I was always around and thought it was creepy or something. Then Hazel...she had the balls to tell you to your face that you needed to back the hell off so she could fuck me in my room whenever she felt like it. We don't want more of that shit, Jared. This whole thing? It fits like a fucking puzzle piece, no matter how weird it may seem to anyone outside looking in. Doesn't it just...make sense?" he points out, pleading with me.

"Do you think you can deal with not knowing which of us is the father?"

I don't know why I keep thinking up every worse-case-scenario here. Maybe I'm just projecting all my worries, hoping Jamie can come up with a decent solution. My gut twists, reminding me that things don't always go as planned. I can't imagine a world where Jamie and I resent each other—it's impossible. Trying to imagine a world without Abi in my arms at night cuts like a sharp blade.

Jamie leans forward, nudging me with his fist. "I can," he says. Any child of yours would be like a child of mine. Can you?"

I nod. He's right. I'd love his kid like my own, in this situation or another. "I feel the same."

" Jamie nods. "So, then..."

"We're good?" The words hang in between us, heavy. This feels like the most momentous conversation and we're both sitting in towels to have it.

"Yeah," he finally agrees. "We're good."

20

ABIGAIL

I press my hand to my lower abdomen, trying to imagine the tiniest of things growing inside me. A baby. Who would've thought?

Even standing in front of my mirror doesn't seem to shake the crazy feeling that I'm living someone else's life right now. It doesn't seem like much - there's barely anything other than bloat going on - but it's funny how I can still tell something's different going on with my body.

I'm finishing putting dressing in my work clothes and slip my shoes on, checking my dresser for a stray hair tie to pull my frizzy mess of hair up off my neck when the doorbell rings.

Jamie and Jared left not even fifteen minutes ago, so I guess that one of them has left something. I open the door with a smile on my face, excited to see my boys again so soon, but the person standing in front of me once I open it is the person I least want to see. Struggling to process the whole scene, I brace myself against the doorframe, feeling like something just knocked the wind out of me. "Cody?" I wheeze. "What the hell are you doing here?"

Even though he knows that I rarely use that kind of language, it doesn't seem to distract him at all as he thrusts a bouquet of slightly wilted roses and baby's breath in my face. "Abigail. God, I've missed you," he says. He smiles as though he's been out of town for work. Everything feels wrong.

"You've missed me," I repeat, shocked. How does he have the audacity to say that after what he put me through? How does he have the nerve to even come to my apartment?

I look around, not wanting anyone to see him here

I'm baffled. Is he here to apologize? What does he think, that a few soft words will change things? Even if I wasn't pregnant I'd be telling him to get away from me. My insides churn as much from anger as from sickness. I'm about to tell him to go when he pulls out a box of chocolates and a small black box.

I take a step back. He opens it to reveal the same engagement ring I had my friend Bailey give back to him a few days after the engagement party disaster.

"This is yours, Abigail. It's not meant to be in a box, it's meant to be on your finger. I made a mistake. A really stupid mistake but I promise I won't do it again. Marry me, Abigail. Marry me and I'll do everything I can to make it up to you."

His expression is smug as though he's expecting me to fall into his arms and forget about everything. He thinks that I still love him. That I still want him.

What I want to do it kick him right in the face.

Better still, laugh. The man is delusional. It's all too much. Before I get a chance to say anything, he slips past me. I'm so stunned by all of the past sixty seconds, that I can only look on, disoriented, as he plops the flowers and chocolates down haphazardly onto the coffee table. Somewhere in the back of my brain, I recall that the coffee table was something we went and brought together.

"You don't mind if I come in so we can talk, right?" he asks, even though he's already inside. Good ol' Cody. Always just assuming his way.

He walks right up to me, holding out the opened box, the ring's diamonds glinting under the light.

I take a step back, not wanting to have anything to do with the stupid thing, or Cody, for that matter. His blue eyes widen and do the thing that I used to love, where they crinkle in the corners as he smiles. I grit my teeth, willing myself not to be stupid.

"God, Abigail, if you only knew what was going on inside my head. It was cold feet...I kept thinking that maybe I was just unsure about committing to you. I didn't want to marry you at the wrong time and then potentially ruin your life later on. I just—"

But I hold up my hand, already feeling the sting of his empty words that only sound pretty. "Nope. It's my turn. You literally had three years to figure all that out already, Cody," I say, counting to three on my fingers. "Do I need to say it again? Three. Years. And let's not forget, you're the one who proposed to me, remember? If you weren't sure about committing, then why in the world did you think it was a good idea to ask me to marry you? Ah-ah,

I'm not done," I quickly add, refusing to let him get a word in. "You've always had a nasty habit of flaking out on all of our plans. I just never thought our actual relationship would be one of them. And now you're here with the ring...like it's going to convince me to go back to you. Is that what you think?"

Cody drops his gaze to the floor, and for the first time in recent memory, he actually looks pretty guilty. I mentally smack myself in the head. Nope, not going to fall for it.

"I understand, but maybe if you just give us another chance, we can fix this. I can fix this. We owe it to ourselves, don't you think?"

This time I really do smack myself in the forehead, lightly. "No, I don't think."

"Okay, okay. I mean like, not right away. Just...over time. You remember how things were between us...well, we can get that back."

I suddenly hate every single thing I ever said to him to inflate his already too-big ego. It's so unfair of him to just come into my life all over again, trying to make himself sound like he makes sense, with words that should hold more water than they actually do.

"Ugh. I cannot hear stuff like this right now, Cody! This isn't fair to me for you to just waltz in here like this!"

He's like a shark with the scent of blood dripping one tiny drop at a time—he rushes right in to take advantage. "Oh, come on, Abi. You and I both know we work so well together. All the ways we've been together, it's always been perfect," he croons closer to me and snakes his hand up my arm, trying to rub my shoulder like he used to before we'd go to bed.

I shake his hand off feeling totally creeped out. "No. We're not doing this."

"But if we could just try. You know what? You don't even have to do anything—leave it all to me. I'll grovel if you want, I don't even care anymore, Abi. Babe, I just want to try and work it out with you." There's a definite note of desperation in his voice. It's not often you hear Cody's voice crack from its usual confident tenor.

"Cody, I'm busy. You need to get the heck out. Now." I point to the front door, impatiently.

"Okay. I'll come back. I get that you're busy."

"Get out, Cody," I say through gritted teeth, unable to care less whether this hurts his feelings or not. Shoving at him, I finally get the point across, and Cody laughs as if it's all just some big joke.

"Okay, I'm gone, I'm gone. Just think about what I said!" he says, that stupid laugh making me only want to physically remove him even more. I practically slam the door shut behind him, locking it and bolting it up just because.

The very last thing I want to think about right now is anything that just came out of Cody's mouth,

My stomach heaves, and I have to make a run for it to the bathroom, emptying the quick breakfast I made for the three of us earlier, into the toilet.

Morning sickness. After seeing Cody and being in his presence, vomiting seems like the only appropriate response.

21

JARED

I never thought I'd see the day where Jamie can't decide between a pink blanket with white hearts or a green blanket with yellow stars.

"This should be illegal. I mean fuck, look at how goddamn adorable this is," he groans, holding up a third choice: a white blanket with little rubber ducks on it. "This is why men don't do the baby shopping stuff."

I roll my eyes at him. "Don't be an ass. You know that hasn't been true for the last thirty years or so. Besides, you have to admit, this is kind of fun." I toss him a giant fluffy white bunny, the floppy ears nearly knocking him over.

"Pfft." There's a small gasp and when I turn back around, Jamie's got two large suction cups over his chest, laughing like some kind of idiot. "Check this out, man!" He turns on the demo model of the breast pump, the sound of it drawing attention from a lady passing by, giving the both of us dirty looks. I flip through the list I made earlier after checking out 'Daddy's No-Bullshit Guide to Babies.'

"Yeah, they do say that breastfeeding is better, but I don't want to put that kind of pressure on Abi if she's not really into it. Maybe we should ask her first on this one."

Jamie snorts, still laughing over the way his shirt is slowly being sucked into the vacuum suctions. "I think this will put plenty of pressure on her. Holy shit, that's going to be hilarious to watch. It'll be like milking a cow...I very sexy cow."

"Do you even hear the words coming out of your mouth?" I ask, shaking my head at him. "You better hope Abi doesn't hear you referring to her that way."

In the end, we decided to get all three blankets because babies apparently piss and crap themselves like crazy so logic. Jamie even put in a request for the ridiculous bunny, citing something about the baby needing a solid collection of stuffed animals to start its life off right. I had to physically remove the breast pump from his hands, though.

"You know, it'll be nice when we don't have to keep referring to the baby as an 'it,'" I tell him as we pull up to Abi's apartment building. "When is she supposed to find out that kind of thing, anyway, I wonder?"

"No idea. Why don't you consult your 'Nerd's Guide to Knocking Up a Chick?'" Jamie nods to the parking space that Abi's car usually occupies, and it hits me that she's working today.

"Oh, right. I forgot she's at Dandies' today. We can just drop everything off at our place, then." He looks back at the piles of baby stuff we've already accumulated as I park the van, a weird expression clouding his face. "You don't think we overdid it, do you? Like, Abi's not going to be pissed, right?"

I glance in the rearview, looking at it all myself. Our mom rarely talks about it now, but we understood it was hard for her as a single mom having to provide for not one, but two kids on her own. There were plenty of birthdays that went by where we only had cake and whatever one toy we wanted to pick out from the discount store.

"Nah. Our kid is going to have whatever it needs. Simple as that." I'm just about to pull away from the curb when something catches my eye. "Hey, do you see that shutter over there?" I ask, pointing toward the apartments again.

"Shutter? What the hell?" Jamie follows my line of sight. "What, at Abi's?"

I frown, staring at the slightly crooked thing. "It looks off."

"No, no, no. You're full of shit. I fixed that a few days ago,   man."
I shrug. "Well, then you did a shitty job. I'm going to go fix it real quick." I pull back over to the front of the building, and throw the van into park, yanking open the back door to grab my tool bag. "I told you you'd need those longer screws, jackass."

"Motherfucker..." Jamie mumbles, following after me up   the   path   to   Abi's. After unscrewing all the too-short for shit screws, I toss them into the bag and pull out the right size, Jamie pretty much fuming as I hand him one. "Make sure to get it in there good."

We set to work and in no time flat, we have the shutter in a level position. I stand back, admiring the work.

"Yeah, well that's all well and good, but you're forgetting something," Jamie suggests, an obvious smugness in the way he shrugs at me.

"Please do tell," I sigh.

"Probably should seal it up. Just for good measure."

And of course, he'd say that—it's kind of known that he has a steadier hand for it than I do.

Naturally, he picks up the caulking gun with a smirk.

"Better?" I ask, rolling my eyes at how deliberately slow Jamie's moving.

He looks back at me from over his shoulder. The grin says it all. Bastard.

The grass behind us rustles too loudly for it to be the breeze, and we both turn at the same time to see none other than Cody standing there awkwardly, clearly debating on whether he's going to say anything or not. His eyes widen slightly.

The red that bleeds into my vision goes hazy, and my hands are grabbing fistfuls of this asshole's shirt, ready to beat him to a bloody pulp. All the things he did to Abi, the way he did her wrong...and then Jamie's shoving me backward, yanking me until I can't move more than a foot away.

"What the fuck are you doing here, Cody?" Jamie spits.

"I was passing and saw you fixing up Abi's place. I just wanted to thank you for looking after my girl and all. I know Abi and I haven't been doing so good but that's all gonna change."

Jamie has to yank me even harder at the mention of 'my girl.' I'm ready to fucking explode.

"You dumb motherfucker! Who the hell do you think you are?" I scream at him, spit flying out of the corners of my mouth.

"You don't need to be like that. Abi and I are going to work things out and then we're gonna be family."

"You can fuck straight off," I growl, finally shoving away from Jamie as I get a better grip on myself.

"Get the fuck outta here," Jamie adds, nodding his chin in the other direction.

The dumbass has the nerve to look mollified. "I already talked to Abi and she wants us to work things out too."

"See?" Cody points through the barely-open curtains to where a small bunch of flowers and a red heart-shaped box lay on the coffee table. "I was here this morning but she had to go to work."

A wall goes up in my mind, blocking it all off. "I don't believe you. She'd never go back to your pathetic ass."

I can tell Cody wants so badly to say something in retaliation but he's not a total idiot. He knows he has no ground here, and he'd easily have his ass handed to him. "You don't have to believe me. It's the truth, though." He sounds downright giddy for someone who just got rejected by Abi. I look back in the window. Jamie and I didn't get those for her so how else would they have shown up? He has to be telling the truth at least about being here earlier.

I pull at Jamie's sleeve. "Let's get out of here. We'll talk to her about it later, once she's home. I turn back to face Cody. "And you need to get the hell out of here too, or else I'll call the police. I don't think they'd be too fond of the mayor's son showing up on his ex's doorstep against her wishes. That's stalker behavior."

Cody throws up his hands in surrender but doesn't get rid of the slightly smug look on his face. "No problem. I'll just talk to her, myself."

We wait until he's down the road a fair bit before we head back to our place.

"He's just full of shit, man," Jamie says as we cross the road. "Abi's too smart to listen to his bullshit."

My brother sounds completely confident but I'm not so sure. Either Cody's an excellent liar or there's something going on here. The thought of Abi talking to that piece of shit and potentially listening to his crap makes me want to break things.

22

JARED

Dandies' wasn't so busy today, but my feet sure could use the break anyway. *Feet shouldn't get swollen this early in pregnancy, should they?* I wonder aloud as I trudge up the walkway home.

To my surprise, my doorstep is littered with red and yellow roses, and a little basket off to the side where I can already see my favorite coffee shop gift card sticking up out of it. Red and yellow roses? I peer closer, picking up and weighing the basket in my hand.

A little cream-colored envelope is tucked behind the gift card, but I save it for last, investigating what all is inside. My favorite perfume. A small bag of my favorite candy, not to mention the solid chocolate heart wrapped in pink foil. Someone's clearly trying to butter me up—all my favorite things are nestled in tissue paper and the flowers are even freshly cut.

I sigh as I slide my finger under the flap of the envelope, a weird sense of dread permeating everything. *'Richland Park Gazebo. See you there.'*

The handwriting looks like it's purposefully trying to throw me off unless there's a fourth so-called suitor waiting in the wings I just don't know about. I shake my head at the thought—that's the kind of stuff soap operas are made out of – but then again, what is my life now, if not some daytime soap opera?

The curve of the letters isn't very familiar to me, but thinking about it now, I haven't had that many chances to really get a good look at Cody's handwriting over the past three years and forget Jared's or Jamie's.

I pause for a moment, the gazebo mentioned, suddenly flickering into view as I close my eyes. It just so happens to be the very same place Cody proposed to me, well, at least the first time, anyway. I chew on my lip and step over the roses to unlock my front door, careful not to mess any of them up.

But the gift seems much more thoughtful than the stunt he pulled earlier this morning, and two attempts in one day are more effort than Cody's ever put forth before.

The Richland Park gazebo is known to be a pretty romantic place, so maybe the twins got the idea in their head and it's all just a big coincidence? They're much more adept at this kind of thing, I can already tell. I mean, shopping, cleaning, repairing things for me? Way more than anything Cody ever did.

Tucking the note back into my pocket, I slip into my sandals and let my hair down, giving myself one last look-over before finding a vase for the flowers. No, this isn't Cody. This has to be Jamie and Jared.

With the basket in hand, I make the fifteen-minute walk down to Richland Park, fidgeting with the handle on the basket the whole time, nervousness flooding through me. "Don't be stupid, Abi," I whisper to myself, glad no one's around. "There's nothing to be nervous about."

The pine needles crunch under my feet as I walk up the little bike path that curves around the outer edges of the park, each step giving me more confidence. I don't know what Jamie and Jared have in mind, bringing me here to the gazebo.

There's no one there when I arrive, so I stroll up to it and run my hand along the rounded curve of the railing, taking in the green scenery of the park. It's actually a beautiful day. They picked a good time to do, well, whatever they're going to do.

I barely have a chance to react to the sound of the footsteps moving quickly across the old wooden floor of the gazebo when warm hands close over my eyes, someone's breath in my ear. "I'm so glad you made it."

Whirling around, confused, I nearly knock him right over. He reels back and rubs at his jaw, irritation flashing across his face before he smooths it over.

"Hey, babe."

23

JAMIE

"You could try being a little more inconspicuous, you know."

Tearing my gaze away from the window, waiting for Abby to get home, I throw a look over my shoulder at Jared. "Oh, shut the hell up. We've both been itching to go over and show her everything, and you know it. Don't try and pretend."

The living room is jam-packed with our huge haul of baby stuff from earlier today. A crib being the centerpiece of it all. Everything else is stuffed all around it, shoved into big white bags.

While we had the day off though, Abi worked, and any moment now, she'd be coming home. It's probably stupid, but I'm stoked to see her reaction to all the things we got. Even if we did go just a tiny bit overboard.

Jared accidentally knocks one of the towers of diapers over as he skirts by it, cursing under his breath. Okay, that may be an understatement, after all...

I look back out the window just in time to see Abi's little car pull into her space. "She's home, man." "Okay," he calls from somewhere down the hall. "At least give her some time to relax before you go barging in over there."

I raise both of my middle fingers and direct them at my brother, even though he can't exactly see them through the walls.

Pulling open the blinds, I watch as Abi stops short at her door, picking what looks like some kind of container—a basket, maybe? off the ground. I'm pretty sure there's a smile that spreads across her face as she looks through the basket of stuff, but it's a little hard to tell from all the way over here.

If I didn't know any better, I'd guess that Jared put together the basket, but he's been too busy to do anything without me knowing.

"Hey. Hey!" I call out to him, refusing to look away from the window, even when Abi steps inside.

"What?" Jared asks over the sound of running water. "Who died, bro?"

I'm still staring out the window when a minute later, Abi steps back outside and gathers up what looks like a bunch of roses from this angle, sticking them carefully into a tall blue vase. She pulls her door shut behind her and with the mystery basket in tow, Abi walks down the path that leads to the main sidewalk.

"Well? Look! Where do you think she's going with that?" I ask him as he comes to see what's up. "It's a basket. And not just any basket...it came with a shit ton of flowers too. Please tell me you had that all delivered to her and just forgot to mention it to me."

Jared pushes his way to get a better view, his eyes narrowing as Abi walks out of sight. "No gift basket from us, no."

Something cold and scaly curls up inside my gut. If it wasn't us, then maybe.

"That motherfucker's trying to win her back," I tell Jared.

Jared meets my eyes. The blood is slowly draining from his face, too. I don't need to hear him say it, to know he's thinking the same as me. " But...Abi doesn't want any part of him. Why would she be strolling off with that basket."

"Is she going to meet him?" I ask even though I know Jared has no more idea about what the hell is going on than I do.

Jared shrugs. "I don't know, but I think we need to find out. At the very least we can keep the asshole from trying to pull anything with her."

"You think we should follow her?"

"Don't you?" he asks. "She's carrying our baby, dude. We gotta look out for her."

"I don't think she'd see it that way."

Jared shrugs again, already heading towards the door. "Then we better make sure she doesn't see us."

It doesn't take us very long to catch up with her, realizing that she's heading to Richmond Park, and by the time she edges around the bike path, we're close enough to hold back a little. It feels stupid, us having to hide like this, but I don't want her thinking we're being possessive jerks or something. Hell...maybe we are.

"Look, look," Jared hisses a minute later, tilting his chin toward the end of the path where it spirals up to the gazebo. Abi's standing there, alone, the basket swinging back in forth in her hand. We both jump back behind the covering of trees when she swivels in our direction.

When I peek back around at her, she's looking across the park.

And then I see him.

Him and his idiotic fucking goofy grin, absolutely pleased with himself as he goes up the steps to the gazebo. I elbow Jared hard and we both watch on as Cody has the fucking nerve to put his hands on Abi's soft face, covering her eyes. The moment he leans in to whisper against her ear, I know I'm going to fucking lose it. Seeing him earlier at her apartment was nothing compared to this.

The murderous thoughts that rummage through my head are all now firing forth in a straight line, all of them directed at him.

Jared's pulling at my arm, whispering for me to stop being a prick, and pushing me to keep walking. I want to look back. I need to look back. But I can't do it-- I just can't fucking do it. All the things we told her and all the things she said right back to us...it's like it was just a dream. I grit my teeth and walk faster, not even bothering to see if my brother is catching up or not. I just need to be as fucking far away from here as I can get, as fast as I can get there.

The neighborhoods blur by. I don't even know when I started to run, but I'm panting by the time I get back to our place, leaning up against my truck for balance. I wish I could forget everything I just saw...

"Jamie."

I shake my head. I don't want to have this fucking conversation.

"Jamie, c'mon, man. Let's just go inside."

I shove away from the truck bed, storming inside our house until I've got nothing left to do but pace the kitchen floor. I know Jared's going to come in and try to make some sense of this shit, but it's impossible. The situation is totally fucked.

"If this is what Abi wants then...well, we can't do anything about it. It's her choice," he says finally, waiting until my pacing slows.

But... "Yeah, well, that's Abi's choice. But she's carrying my baby. Or your baby. *Our* baby. And no matter what she wants to do, we have *every* damn right to be a part of our kid's   life."

--

The TV does nothing to distract me from everything that's happened. And Jared...well, he's just as dazed as I am. Slouching against the back of the couch, his eyes constantly darting between the car chase scene of the movie and the half-opened blinds.

I've lost track of time, but it doesn't seem like it's been that long before Jared sits up, pushing the blinds back even more. Finally, he looks at me and nods.

"She's back."

I take a deep breath, not unlike Jared, and try to lay the cards out in front of us as if that's going to make it any easier..."We need to tell her we know. There's no point in beating around the damn bush with her. She wanted honesty. She's fucking getting it. But...are we sure we can have this conversation with her yet?"

Jared drops his gaze. "Honestly? I don't really know."

Ever since we came to terms with the fact that Abi was pregnant, it only seemed natural for us to do the stupid dad things like arguing over baby names, imagining the sports our kid would play, and what they'd look like. We've already planned out the next eighteen years in the short span of time, and here it is, being ripped right out from underneath us.

This whole thing was supposed to be perfect. Yeah, it was going to be hard with our parents and all, but we were going to make it work somehow.

I grit my teeth, ready to rip the fucking band-aid off. The last thing I'm going to do is do nothing.

"We don't have a choice. We need to tell her, and we need to tell her now."

Jared nods slowly. "I guess we'll just leave everything here. For now."

I don't dare look at the mountain of baby things we bought first thing this morning. It already hurts enough to breathe. "Yeah. For now."

24

ABIGAIL

My hand still stings after slapping the hell out of Cody's face the moment he tried to force me to kiss him back under the gazebo. He was mad. I guess I never said no to him before about anything. It felt so damn good. When he realized that I wasn't going to accept his proposal and there was nothing he could say to make me change my mind, he got nasty.

"You know I was seeing someone else while we were together," he snarls. "That's why I didn't turn up to the engagement. I was with her."

He thinks that telling me this now is going to hurt me but if anything it does the opposite. It cements what I already thought I knew; that Cody is worthless and nasty and I am so completely better off without him.

He's lucky I didn't sic Dad on him.

I'm tempted to now.

I was going to relax after working on my feet all day, but after dealing with Cody's skeevy moves, all I really want to do is to crawl into bed and pass out. Preferably with my boys. Just the thought of snuggling up between their broad chests calms me down, and it's all I can do to keep from running over there.

I check my hair in the mirror, tugging my fingers through it to try and remove at least some of the knots, and shove my keys into my pocket. I make it all the way across the street to where the truck's parked, and see Jared and Jamie slowly walking out of the house wearing completely unreadable expressions on their matching faces. They look really pissed at something.

"Hey." I give them a little wave and plaster on a smile. Ugh, I can still smell Cody's copious amounts of heavy aftershave as if he's still right next to me, breathing in my ear. Hopefully, they won't catch a whiff.

My smile disappears, though when they turn their grim expressions on me. I don't know what it is yet, but my skin prickles. "What's wrong?"

Jamie's eyes narrow carefully at me as he's very obviously working on what he wants to say, so as usual,

Jared's the first to speak up. "If you wanted to get back together with Cody, you should have told us."

I stare at him. "What? What are you talking about?"

Jamie's thick biceps flex as he folds his arms across his chest. "We saw you two, Abigail," he says, my full name sounding utterly wrong coming from him. "We know he went by to see you this morning because we ran into him. The smug bastard went on about how things were going to work out between you. We thought he was full of shit and that you'd set him straight but then you plan some sort of meet up with him in the park."

I know that there's a stronger point here to make, but I keep imagining Jamie and Jared secretly following me around without my knowledge. They...they wouldn't! Would they?

"How do you know about that?" I can barely bring my voice above a whisper.

"We saw you, Abi."

"You were in the park?" I ask.

For a second Jared looks sheepish, and I know. They followed me and at least Jared has the decency to look embarrassed about it.

"So you're getting back with him?" Jamie says, his voice low and angry.

I take a step back. "I can't believe you two," my voice shakes. "Had you done the responsible and *respectable* thing and just waited until I came to you, you'd know that I had no idea it was Cody I was meeting up with in the park, I thought it was you. But you think it's okay to spy on me without even letting me know you're there!" My stomach roils but I swallow it back. "You two must think I'm some naïve idiot if you think I'd ever take Cody back. Even if things hadn't happened with the three of us, I'd never in a million years want to be with Cody again." I level my gaze with them, not backing down as they both look away, embarrassed. Irritation prickles across my skin.

Jamie reaches out to me, clasping his hand around my elbow, his eyes wide. "I'm sorry, Abi." His eyes dart between me and his brother. "We...jumped to some conclusions."

Jared takes a few steps closer to us. "We're the idiots. And you're right, we shouldn't have done something so immature. We just couldn't stand the thought of him trying to manipulate you again."

"I can handle myself, Jared." I take in a deep breath, suddenly unsure about everything. Relief is written across their faces, but I'm not ready to just make nice. I start pacing back and forth alongside the truck. It's like I want to jump out of my own skin. "Cody never trusted me. He was always worried that I would cheat on him, or leave him for someone else. Maybe it's because he knew he was a terrible boyfriend and he was doing those things himself, I don't know. Funny how he turned out to be the one cheating...," I say. "And then when I told him I was pregnant, he tried to get back down on his knees, literally begging me for me to take him back. I told him there was no way in hell I'd let him raise my child that wasn't even his, to begin with, and he had the nerve to call me a slut. He'll probably be wearing that nice handprint on his face for the next few days if I had to guess."

"That motherfucker. We knew he probably ran around on you, the way he carried on..." Jamie hisses.

I hold up my hand so he shuts up. "That doesn't excuse any of what you did, though, and I don't think it's smart to head into another relationship like that with someone—let alone two someones! I refuse to be thought of and treated that way again."

Jamie's shaking his head, panic clear as crystal on his face, while Jared gets closer to me again, meeting my eyes. "Abi, please, it's not like that at all. We trust you. It's Cody we didn't trust. We saw him and he said you were getting back together. We were worried that he was putting pressure on you and that you might feel like you owed him a second chance. You're having our baby." He says the last bit and looks around as though he's worried who might be catching bits of our conversation. "Can you just...can you please come inside?" He gestures to the house behind him. "Let's talk in private."

"I don't know," I say. "I don't really have anything else to say."

"But we do," Jamie says. "We've got plenty to tell you and show you."

The truth is that as much as I want to keep being mad about all this, I feel so damned tired all of the sudden. Too much is happening in my life right now and it's overwhelming. "All right," I sigh. I desperately want us to work things out but I wasn't lying when I said I refuse to be treated like that.

But the idea of talking more dies when I step inside their house that looks less like a bachelor pad and more like a baby-registry come to life.

There are huge piles of bags all around their living room, filled to the brim with baby things, blankets, stuffed animals, clothes, even pacifiers from what I can see overflowing. Not to mention the two large boxes of the two smallest sized diapers. In the middle of the assortment of bags are huge boxes with pictures of a fancy stroller, a 3-in-1 changing table, and a gorgeous cherrywood-colored crib. All the kinds of things that a proud first-time dad would get, and then some.

I blink once, twice, and again. My eyes well up almost instantly, and something flutters in my chest as I walk up to the nearest bag and pull out the softest fleece blanket with little yellow stars on it. It's not hard to imagine a sweet little baby wrapped up in it, cuddling close against me and while the cautious part of me knows it might be a little soon to get everything prepared like this, I don't even care.

"You...you did all of this? Today?" Mm, the blanket even smells sweet and clean.

Both of them nod solemnly, still waiting.

As I peek into the rest of the bag, catching glimpses of more soft, fluffy blankets, it's like my heart is knocking on my brain's door, telling it to hurry the hell up and get with the program. That the boys mean it—they really do want this.

And I've never felt such happiness and panic swell up inside me like this before.

Spinning around on my feet, I face them, my heart racing at the words tumble out. "I don't know what to say…I'm sorry. I understand why you might have gotten the wrong idea, and it makes sense that you were worried." I hate how I keep tripping over every syllable, my throat dry while my eyes are wet. "And now I just…I never imagined that this could happen…and oh god, it feels like I'm way too close to losing all of it at any second. Like you'll leave me too, and all of it will be gone, like so much else has gone in my life…"

Suddenly, I miss my mom so much. I have a child growing inside me. The grandchild she will never hold and there is so much I wish I could ask her.

Jamie and Jared are close in a flash, arms surrounding me, hands stroking my hair, wiping my tears away. They have me between them, and it's just what I need. Jared softly cups my cheek and I lean into it, my eyes fluttering shut under his touch. Jamie's behind me, his chin on top of my head, listening too.

"You're never, ever going to have to worry about losing us, okay? Jared's eyes are fierce and I want so much to believe him. "We're gonna be with you for every single doctor's appointment, every single weird craving, every backrub you'll need."

Jamie chuckles. "I'm definitely here for any *special* kind of cravings."

Trust him to try and lower the tone. I'm just about to swat at him, sniffing but smiling and his silly humor when the sound of an engine roars along the road. It stops right outside the twins house and two doors slam shut almost immediately. All of us turn to the window just in time to see Natalie storming up to the house with my dad right behind her.

25

JAMIE

Mom is striding towards our front door with the same look on her face as the time that me and Jared set off firecrackers down the sink drain in the tiny apartment we used to live in.

Abi practically flies out the door in hopes of stopping them from seeing everything we have stashed in our living room, and I scramble, helplessly trying to find something—anything—to cover up all of the baby things. There's no way we can move fast enough.

"Shit, shit, shit," I mutter. There are sheets in the linen closet, but how the hell would I explain what was underneath?

Jared's eyes his eyes shift back and forth, clearly in the same mind-frame. There's just no way of making this not seem batshit crazy. Maybe if Abi can distract them.

The door flies open and in storms Mom, her green eyes blazing, and Sam…he stares back over his shoulder as he walks in, this crazy pained expression on his face, his eyes on Abi when she slinks back inside.

Mom immediately spots me and Jared standing awkwardly in front of all the baby things as if we can actually hide all of it behind us. I don't even bother with a guilty smile—there's no getting out of this one.

She pushes past us easily, and brings her hand to her mouth, not covering up the loud gasp that escapes. When she turns back to face Sam, I'm not too sure her head isn't going to explode right off her shoulders.

"Someone better explain to me what the hell is going on, right now," she demands, looking first at us and then at Abi.

"I, uh. We should probably—" Abi begins, shuffling over to us slowly.

"—A rather crazy thing just happened, actually. Your father and I decided to stop for a bite to eat at the diner. My friend Rebecca was on her break and came and told us a little story about Cody running off at the mouth with his buddies at a booth. Apparently, Cody was telling everyone that you were pregnant. I told Rebecca he must have had it wrong, that there was no way… But then Sam's buddy came by to congratulate me on being a grandma, telling us that he and his wife spotted you two," she says, turning back to us with nothing but steel in her eyes, "coming out of the BabiesRUs with cart-fulls."

It feels like she's only a split-second from piecing it all together.

She drops her gaze down to the floor, slowly turning back to face Abi. "Is it true, Abigail? Are you pregnant?"

Abi's lips tremble as she nods, and I can see the way she looks at her dad. I can feel just how crushed he is, and it's almost too much for me to keep watching.

"Is it Cody's?" Sam asks. Abi shakes her head and he looks toward us as if we can fill in the things that Abi isn't saying.

Mom glances around the room, her eyes zeroing in the crib. "Why do you have a house full of baby things?"

Nobody says a word and the silence feels claustrophobic.

"If it's not Cody's, whose is it?"

Seconds tick passed and still, no one says anything. Abi looks as though she might throw up all over our parent's feet. I gently take hold of her by the elbow and help her sit down. When I look back up at Sam, his eyes are narrowed and watchful.

"I am. Pregnant. I am pregnant," Abi repeats, clearing her throat. "But it's still really early. I only just found out." A pang of pride shoots through me. I can only imagine how hard it must be for her.

Mom hesitates before finally asking, "And the father?"

Abi shakes her head. "I don't know."

A strange pained sound leaves Sam's mouth. He turns from Abi as though he can't bear to look at her and I want to shout at him for being this way. Mom looks so shocked too, as though an invisible hand just came in and smacked her across the face. The tension in the room has shot straight through the roof. I'm waiting for the eruption that seems inevitable.

"What do you mean you don't know," Sam says lowly.

Abi fiddles with her fingers, avoiding everyone's gaze. "I mean that I don't know for sure," she says.

"I can't believe this of you, Abi," Mom says, shaking her head in total disbelief. "This is not the way your father raised you."

I know she's our mother, but hearing her talk to Abi like that makes me want to put my fist through the wall.

"Mom," Jared says in a warning tone.

"What?" mom hisses. "I'm only saying what everyone will think."

"I don't care what everyone things," I say, taking a step forward so that Abi is behind me and shielded from this. "Abi's an amazing woman who has her head on straight despite what you're insinuating and she needs our support, not our judgment."

Sam takes a few steps closer to the weird crowd of us in front of the baby items, but he's looking between me and my brother. "Why do you have a room full of baby things?" he asks. I guess he's realized we never answered our Mom the first time the question was asked.

I glance at Jared and Abi, their expressions equally as torn as I know mine must be. We could keep it a secret, at least for a while longer, but still, everyone will eventually need to know the truth. If we lie to our parents now, it is going to make everything so much worse in the long run. The circumstances are not ideal, however you look at it, and the way our parents have come to hear about the news of the baby is awful.

There is no changing any of this, though. We are where we are.

We love Abi and I think she loves us, and although that baby is as tiny as a kidney bean, we all love it too.

I nod at my brother and Abi. Their eyes widen when they realize what I'm trying to tell them.

It's time to get it over with.

"We bought the baby things," I say, trying to keep my voice even. "We bought them to show Abi how serious we are about our baby."

Seconds tick past and I start to wonder if I actually said that out loud or just in my head.

Sam's eyes widen more like he can't quite see what's in front of him, and my Mom's blinking so fast I know she can't. A dry sob escapes her throat and she shakes her head, looking completely bewildered. "I. I…What?" Her mouth opens and shuts repeatedly.

"The baby is ours," I say again.

Abi's eyes are on the floor, her face flushed. Jared is staring at me as though he can't quite believe this is happening. I'm never the one who keeps my head in situations like this. I'm the one who heads in like a bull in a china shop, then has to apologize for the broken wreckage I leave behind. I don't know why I'm managing to keep from shouting this time. Maybe I've finally realized the importance of getting this message across in the right way. I have one chance. I have to do the best for our baby.

"Ours?" Mom says, disbelief raising her voice. "I baby can only be made by one man and one woman, Jamie. Are you saying that you…?" She doesn't finish the sentence but looks between us to answer anyway.

"The baby could belong to either of us."

Sam makes a strangulated sound. "You slept with both of them?"

Abi looks at him in horror. This is definitely not the kind of conversation you want to have with your father.

"Is that what you're saying?" Mom hisses at me.

I nod.

She brings up her hand and points a trembling finger at me. I can see how livid she is. "I never thought I say this to you but I am disgusted. What the hell do you think you are all doing? We're a family. This isn't what you do in a family."

"We're not related to Abi, Mom," Jared says softly.

"You're related to your brother," she shouts. "You slept with your stepsister, and so did your brother. Do you not see how many levels of wrong this is?"

I glance across at Sam who looks as though he's struggling to keep it together.

"I'm so ashamed," Mom says and I get a knot in my stomach. Those are words I've never heard from her before and I feel her disappointment. I knew this was going to hurt them. None of it is as we would have planned it, but I love Abi and I'm not prepared to be ashamed of our child.

Jared opens his mouth to say something but I put my hand up. I started this so I'm going to finish it, whatever the outcome.

"We love Abi," I say, looking directly at Sam. I need him to know this. I need him to see that we plan to stand by his daughter and grandchild. "We love her and we're happy about the baby. It may not be the ideal set up in the eyes of society, but we're not going to hurt the people we love to fit in."

"You've hurt me," she spits. "You've hurt Sam. He took us into his home…"

Those words hang in the air and I hate to admit it but I do feel shame. She's right. He trusted us and in his eyes, we've betrayed him.

"We love Abi," I say again as though love has the power to make everything okay.

"Well, you shouldn't," Sam says. His voice sounds hoarse and his eyes are deadened. He shakes his head.

"Dad..." Abi says softly but he puts his hand up to stop her.

He looks between me and Jared, his jaw ticking with anger. For a moment I think he's going to try and lay me out but he doesn't. Sam turns and walks out the door and mom hurries after him, turning back to us as she heads through the front door. "You did this," she says, her eyes filled with tears.

We watch as they get into the car. Neither of them seems to say anything as Sam gets the car into gear and drives away, leaving the three of us in their wake.

26

JARED

Jamie's breathing fast like he just ran a marathon, and Abi looks like she's about to pass out. All I can do is shut the front door, and exhale.

The light's already starting to leak away from the sky, turning half of it a deeply-tinted magenta. It's funny how such a beautiful thing can come right after something so ugly.

Debating on whether I should take her hand or not, I decide to sit down on the couch. We had the day off today, but I feel exhausted. The excitement of buying things for the baby has all but worn off, and all I see in the middle of the living room now is the look on my mom's face when Jamie told her the truth about us and Abi.

Fuck.

I don't even swear internally very much but there isn't any other word that can convey what I'm feeling. Jamie slides down onto the couch next, all the usual confidence and energy gone out of him. We both seem to turn our heads to Abi.

"Well, that went well," she says and then bursts out laughing. I think she's in shock and I look across at Jamie who shrugs and starts laughing too. "Seriously."

"I actually thought that Jamie did a surprisingly good job," I mumble.

Abi nods, putting her face in her hands. "The look on my dad's face. I felt like I was going to wither up."

"He's really pissed," Jamie agrees.

"It was never going to be an easy conversation," I say. "But I think it might have been better if they hadn't heard the news via the town gossips.

They both nod, groaning at the thought. "Trust Cody to go shooting his mouth off."

"That's Cody's area of expertise," Jamie says.

Abi groans again. "I shouldn't have told him but I couldn't get him to understand that I wasn't going to get back with him."

I put my hand on hers. "They had to find out sometime," I say.

"And it's hardly like me and Jared were the stealthiest men on the block," Jamie says. "Going baby shopping...what were we thinking?"

He's right of course. We should have all been a more cautious but our shopping spree was for a good reason. We wanted Abi to see how we felt about the baby. We wanted her to know we're committed.

"They're going to be upset for a while. They both will. But they'll eventually have to come to terms with it," I reply. I half believe it, but I know it's what Abi needs to hear right now.

"Natalie probably hates me now. I've corrupted her perfect sons."

Both Jamie and I snort. "You don't have to blame yourself for that," he says. "There were quite a few corrupting influences that came around before you." He wiggles his eyebrows and Abi chokes out a laugh.

"I'm being serious," she says. "I know how close the three of you are and I couldn't stand the idea of being the thing that comes between you and her." Abi brings her arm down over her face, burying her eyes in the crook of her elbow.

"What are we going to do?" she mumbles.

I turn to face her, wanting to move mountains just to make her feel good again. I draw her arm away so she has to look at me. "We're going to do what we planned. This doesn't change anything, Abi. We're having a baby and as much as that fact might disgust our parents, it's coming anyway. We're gonna do what we were planning to do, except now we don't have to dread coming clean. They know and we can just get on with it."

"And you don't need to worry about coming in between us and our mom. She may be...unreachable right now, but it's not like she's going to disown us," Jamie says.

"Pfft." She folds her arms across her chest. "I'd be careful before you make any more assumptions," she replies.

I take her hand in mine and rub small circles on the back of her hand with my thumbs. "Me and Jamie have always admired you. You have this strength that most people don't seem to give you enough credit for. And you're always honest, but still kind about the truth. You never intentionally hurt others, and you have a pure heart. I know this whole thing really hurt you, and I'm sorry you're having to go through all this but you know we're always going to be here to help make it a little more bearable wherever we can."

Jamie steps up to the plate. "Yeah, absolutely. And Abi, you're going to be like the most amazing mom, because like Jared said, you're pretty much a badass. We know what a strong woman looks like—we lived with one for most of our lives. And don't worry about Mom or your Dad. They'll come around. And you'll see then—everything will all turn out okay in the end."

"Even if we can't get them to accept everything during the pregnancy, I bet things will change once the baby's born. They'll take one look at their first adorable grandkid and put on the blinders. The kid will win 'em over by its supreme cuteness, and then this will feel like a distant memory," I add.

Abi's shoulders seem to relax a little as she nods. "Maybe."

Her eyes are shining, but the tears don't fall. I push a stray wave of copper behind her ear, still in awe of just how beautiful she really is. It's not our fault we fell for Abi when we met her. How could we not, with these eyes and that soft hair?

Jamie rubs her knee, his fingers looking like their itching for more of her. He leans down, kissing her quietly, before she returns the kiss fully, placing her hand on the side of his scruffy face.

I slip my hands under the fabric of her shirt around to her abdomen, holding her as I kiss around the nape of her neck. The chills that explode across her pale skin trigger something inside of me, and I twist her hair out of the way, peppering either side of her neck with slow, deliberate kisses, patiently waiting my turn.

Then suddenly she stops. "You said you love me," she whispers. "You said it to dad." Her eyes are fixed on Jamie but then she turns to me.

"You know how we feel," I say softly.

She shakes her head. "I didn't know that," she says. "I knew you cared for me, but love?"

"From the first day we met you at that restaurant, we had a thing for you," Jamie says. "We used to argue about who was gonna make a move on you, then we were all living in the same house and you didn't seem interested and it just didn't seem like it was ever going to happen for either of us."

"But we got to know you, Abi," I tell her. "Every family meal and night in front of the TV. We were soaking you up."

"Love is a big word," Jamie says. "But we mean it, honey. We loved you before you agreed to marry Cody but neither of us was prepared to admit it because you didn't seem to see us."

"I saw you," she says softly. "The first photograph was enough to drive me crazy."

I snort. "Was it the one of us dressed in suits for our uncle's wedding?"

She nods, grinning. "You both looked so serious."

"We were channeling our inner bad boys," Jamie says. "Mom loves that photo."

"I love it too," Abi says. "I wanted you both so much but I thought I was going crazy. What kind of person wants to be with two men at the same time?"

"A greedy one," Jamie quips an Abi punches him on the shoulder.

"Greed is not a bad thing," I add.

Abi grins. "You love me," she says happily.

"We've established that," Jamie says. "What we haven't established is how you feel about us."

"You don't know," she asks.

We both shake our heads. I mean, I know she's attracted to us, and I think she likes us, but as Jamie said, love is a big word.

"I love you both," she says, putting her hands on our knees. "I can't believe you didn't know."

"You were planning to marry Cody a few weeks ago," Jamie says.

Abi shakes her head. "I loved you, but I couldn't see a way for it to be anything other than a dream."

"Looks like your dream has come true," I say.

"It feels like that," she says and my heart skips a beat. "But I don't want our parents to hate us because of it."

"We can't change the way they feel right now. They're shocked...angry, but in time they'll see that what we've said is true. They'll understand that this is something good and they'll accept it."

"I hope so," Abi says.

"We all do," Jamie adds.

27

ABIGAIL

Jamie's stubble grazes against my neck as he slowly dips his head down to taste my skin, his hands splaying out and around my upper arms, holding me close. I sigh, tilting my head back to give him better access, all the while, Jared's hand slide further up my shirt until he's tracing the swell of my breasts.

They're bigger than they ever have been before, swollen because of the pregnancy. They seem to be growing at the same rate as my bump.

Jared pulls back slightly, searching my face. "Is this okay?" he asks.

But Jamie's already set a motion in plan, scooping me up into his arms as if I weigh nothing. "You know our girl never says no," he says as he carries me down the hall.

Jamie places me down on the bed, Jared quick to follow us. Jared slowly lifts my shirt up and over my head, wasting no time in unhooking and sliding down my bra, freeing my breasts, my nipples standing out in protest against the chilly air.

Jamie pushes my pants down, and hooks his fingers into the waistband of my panties, pulling until I'm able to step out of them. I can see the hunger in both of their eyes, but they're more concerned with taking care of me first, as they always are.

"Can…Can I?" I ask gently, placing my hands on their hips. "I just need to see you right now."

"We're yours, Abi," Jamie says, while Jared nods. They both hold their breath as bite my lip.

I don't say a word, I just get to work, one slow, deliberate movement at a time. The shirts are off first, and I take my time in running my hands along their broad chests, committing every curve of muscle, every dip between the ribs, that I can to memory. It amazes me to see the way they are so very much the same but so very different at the same time.

Jared's abdomen trembles when I undo the button of his jeans and carefully unzip them, while Jamie holds his breath when I do the same to him.

When all that's left is them in their boxer briefs, I take a step back and smile. They watch me watching them, and it sends a thrill down between my legs.

"Take them off," I whisper. I want to see them both at the same time.

Jared is slow with his movement, his gaze never leaving mine as he pushes his underwear down, standing back up with a quiet sort of confidence. On the other hand, Jamie shoves them down his thighs instantly, lit up with excitement from his head to his toes and definitely everywhere between.

I think I understand how lottery players must feel when they've won the jackpot. I can't believe how lucky I am. Even after all these months, I still feel like pinching myself. None of this feels real to me. How often do dreams come true? I feel so blessed to have these men in my life.

My breathing feels shallow as their eyes sweep over my body. The corner of Jared's mouth just barely quirks up. I take the time to really look at him, no need to rush. Smooth tan skin over just the right amount of lean muscle. Thick thighs and strong calves and an ass that I just have to dig my fingers in to. A broad chest that is just perfect for me to rest on and listen to his heart beating.

I look across to Jamie and map him out too. Gorgeous eyes and the cheekiest grin you ever saw. Slightly broader shoulders than his brother and a little more bulk to his biceps too. I love how narrow his waist seems and the dark patch of hair around his cock that gives me so much pleasure.

"She's comparing us," Jamie says.

"Yeah, she is," Jared agrees.

They start to move towards me and shiver runs down my spine. So much man. So much strength, and gentle power.

Jared moves behind me to pull my curls down out of the messy bun on my head until they bounce around my shoulders. I breathe them in, the scent of them making me feel lightheaded. His hands massage right under my head and on either side of my neck, loosening the muscles and sending any tension I was holding packing.

"Mm," I moan, not able to recall the last time someone rubbed my neck like this.

I can't even bring myself to say anything, but I smile still with my eyes closed

Jamie runs his hands along my hips, holding me in place. His lips land first on my shoulder, and then across my neck to the other shoulder, hands slipping back to form a slippery grip on my round hips. He has no qualms letting me feel just how much he wants me, his length pressed firmly against my side.

I'm wet between my legs, and they haven't even touched me yet. Jared's fingers slip between my legs and I gasp softly, my eyes fluttering open to watch his concentration. Jamie's brow furrows as his thumbs just barely rub against my nipples. So much focus on giving me pleasure.

The movements are so careful and deliberate, and I know this is more than them wanting my body. The way they both take their time with me, not rushing even though I'm they want to, tells me how much they love me.

Jamie's hand moves to caress my bump and a lump forms in my throat.

I try not to cry, not wanting to alarm them or anything. The emotion is too much for me sometimes.

They love me and this baby that I'm growing. And I…I'm so in love with them.

I let Jamie push my legs apart, his careful movements with his fingers almost more than I can bear. Reaching up behind me, I cup the side of Jared's face and bring his mouth down to mine, tasting him and drinking him.

He responds slowly at first, but his hands brush over the peaks of my breasts until he's heaving them in his hands, squeezing me. I press back harder against his mouth and he kisses me with even more fervor, his tongue sweep along mine. I can feel his cock stirring against me and it only leaves me wanting more.

Jamie's kneeling down, his tongue finding my clit and licking it gently.

"Ohh," I moan softly. I writhe under him, my breath quickening, feeling the rising pleasure and reveling it in. The get me close but not enough to come. I know what they're doing. Working me into a frenzy so I'll go off like a rocket as soon as one of them pushes inside me.

I'm not complaining.

I love it that way.

When Jared moves deep inside me with one slick movement, I take in a quick shallow breath, moaning like crazy at how full I suddenly feel. His thickness spreads me apart and all it takes is three hard thrusts and I'm gone.

I don't know how you could explain an orgasm to someone who had never had one. The ultimate release, maybe. All I know is that each one I have seems different.

I'm flying as Jared comes inside me. I'm still soaring as Jamie takes his brother's place.

They work as a team, one moving so the other can too, and before I know what's happening, my body is tensing up again, a fire burning and coiling up deep inside me. I let out the cry that seems to cut the air, and try to find purchase on anything, my hands slippery with sweat as I come a second time, stars bursting like fireworks behind my lids.

"Oh, oh god," I moan, more quietly this time. "I love you. I love you both so much."

I hear them both whisper 'I love you' and my heart is fit to burst.

And I know that whatever comes next, I'm never going to have to face it on my own. Jared and Jamie may be my stepbrothers, but they're also my lovers, prepared to take a huge step to be with me and our baby.

All I can do is pray that our parents will one day come to accept us too.

EPILOGUE
ABIGAIL

Eight months later...

The gown fits awkwardly around me, the ties all over the place aggravating the hell out of me. Instead of a lovely dress, though, I'm stuck in this god-awful, itchy hospital gown, wishing I could wear my own. I keep pacing back and forth, and all I can think about is how Jamie and Jared are like, three seconds away from my ultimate wrath if they don't hurry up and get here. Fast.

"How ya feeling, hon?" the nurse asks, shuffling back into the room pushing a small cart.

I suck in a quick breath, assessing everything. Back is killing me. My feet are about the size of two tree trunks waiting for me to trip over them, and my hair is sweaty and plastered on the back of my neck. Oh, and then there's the watermelon that is currently pressing down on my vagina, waiting for the big escape. I don't even bother with the polite smile. "I've been better."

She pats my arm, guiding me back to the side of the hospital bed. "I'm going to go ahead and check to see how things are progressing. And check your blood pressure, of course. Here you go," she says, helping me slide my tree trunks back over. I take a minute to read over her id badge, wondering how stressful it must be to deal with a whole bunch of first-time mothers all day.

"Has anyone heard from my…um, from…"

"Actually, yes. The gentlemen just called the nurse's station. They'll be here shortly."

The cuff nearly cuts off my circulation the more it inflates, and all I want to do is sleep. I'd gone in for an induction only hours ago, and they thought I'd have plenty of time before the contractions would really start to kick in, but when the nurse…Nancy…checked me, I was already dilated to four centimeters. I still can't even wrap my head around *that*.

She goes over the screen, watching the lines as they come in, and presses around the outside of my enormous stomach, nodding to herself. "Oh yes. In the perfect position. Lie back, please, Abigail. You can hold on to the railing if you'd like, hon. I'm just going to go ahead and check how far you are again."

It's uncomfortable but not as bad as the weeks of being prodded and poked while being on bedrest. "Mmkay," I groan as she helps adjust the bed back down.

Gritting my teeth, I wait for her to get on with it, glad once she pulls the gloves off and tosses them into the nearby trash can. "All right, it's looking like you're at a seven now. I know you wanted to wait but if you want the epidural, this is your last chance."

I glance out the window, and then back toward the door, chewing my swollen lip. "I…okay. I really did want to wait for them but…"

The heavy door shoves open on the opposite of the curtain and two huge piles of baby things with strong legs come barreling into my room, nearly knocking into the hospital tray next to my bed.

"Oof!" Jamie sets his arm-full of things down all at once, bottles and pacifiers still in boxes falling out of the tops of tote bags. "I think we got it all."

"Excuse me!" Nancy scolds them, her hands on her plump hips. "There is no need for all the racket—some women are trying to give birth, you know!"

I hide the snicker behind my hand as Jared and Jamie look at the short round nurse, shame clear as day on their faces.

"Sorry, ma'am," Jared says. "We're just…a little excited is all."

"It was your fault, anyway," Jamie turns to his brother, shaking his head. "You just had to make the last pitstop…"

"It was an important one," Jared replies, narrowing his eyes at Jamie. "And plus, if you hadn't taken so long…"

The two of them keep going back and forth while me and Nancy just roll our eyes, and she quickly looks at the screen. "I'm going to go ahead and let the anesthesiologist know to bring your waiver form."

She leaves the three of us alone and still, Jared and Jamie are fighting. I'd usually have patience, but something shifts really low inside of me, and it feels like all of my muscles are tightening way too much around my womb, not unlike the way my arm was nearly suffocated by the blood pressure cuff.

I freeze, wanting to get back up out of the bed but unable to move. "Uh, guys?"

"But I already told you I grabbed the pillow! It's not my fault you take forever to get anywhere..."

I clear my throat, leaning forward to try and pull myself up. Somewhere in the back of my mind, I remember reading about sitting on an exercise ball. Of course, I don't have one here because it's the hospital and not a freaking gym. I take another breath. "Guys."

When neither of them seems to really hear me, I shriek, "Shut the hell up!" That gets their attention fast enough, and they're immediately by my side. "I think this is the big contractions Doctor Ramsey was telling us about..." my voice trails off into a weird groan as it finally lets up. And I'm supposed to deal with this all day?

Luckily for me though, my body is ready for this grueling journey to be over, and the labor that everyone expects to take much longer, lasts for barely more than a couple hours, all the while my guys circle around me, letting me squeeze the ever-loving crap out of their hands. I didn't even make it long enough for the epidural to be administered before I had become fully dilated and they had no choice. The frustration in not having relief was almost as bad as the actual pain, and each time I felt the raw wave of it crashing over me, I looked at one of the guys and screeched. I was so not going to let them forget this.

I'm so lost in my own head and body that I don't even realize Doctor Ramsey has settled between my legs until he instructs Jamie and Jared to each grab my leg to help me push.

I try to brace myself but it's impossible, I feel like I'm losing sight of what all of this was about in the first place, only wanting to hurry up and stop the pain...

The first round of relief hits, and I take a gasping breath as if I've just come up for air. There's a muffled gurgling cry, and my eyes fly open. I can just barely make out little red, wrinkly feet, when another wave of stretching, tearing pain takes over.

"It's a girl! She's a little girl!" Jared says, closer as he leans down and kisses my sweaty forehead, still clinging on to my leg.

"You two grab her legs, let the dads get in there," Doctor Ramsey tells two of the nurses standing by. "You're almost done now, Abigail."

The room is a quiet chaos of baby shrieks and hurried whispers. "Here you go, sir. Would you like the cut the cord?"

A clamp is passed around me and Jamie stands blinkingti as the nurses present the cord for him to cut. I just manage to catch his teary eyes as he does it, and the loud, writhing baby bundled up in a soft white blanket is passed to him carefully.

The pain pulls me back to my body yet again, and I let out a loud sob as Doctor Ramsey tells me to push, push, push. I breathe as deeply as I can and hold it in, giving my body the strength it needs...

"Here we go! Baby B is here! Another girl!"

The total and utter relief I feel takes over everything, but I raise my face to watch as Jared's presented with the second baby's cord to cut, and only moments later, our sweet baby is placed in his arms as well. I want to pull them all up to me so I can keep them all safe from harm, but I'm so tired...

"Here they are, Abi," Jared whispers. "Look at our sweet girls."

I look up to see both my wonderful, loving men on either side of me, both of their arms full of crying baby. The tears that have been streaming down my face are no match for the joy that swells up inside of me.

They're here, and now I have my family.

--

"I still can't get over how tiny their little fingers are," I giggle, a little delirious from the twenty-four hours. "I mean, look at them." I take Elizabeth's hand in mine, trying to learn more about the little bodies I've been growing inside of me.

Jamie peers over us, nodding. "It's so crazy, right? And look, I think she has me and Jared's nose!"

I run my fingers very softly over the tufts of strawberry blonde hair on her tiny head, cataloging all I already know about my children: Elizabeth is older by only two minutes, but she's smaller than Eleanor by over five ounces. Eleanor is the calm one, her eyes already studying everything around her, while Elizabeth is wiggly and makes the funniest faces. And they both look so much like their daddies, but I can see bits of me in there, too.

I sigh. Bits of me...and bits of Dad. The moment I'd been dreading trickles in and my eyes blur as the tears well up. This whole time I had to brave this thing with only Jared and Jamie's help. Of course, my friends and even Dandie were very helpful and very sweet.

But without Dad and Nat accepting everything and wanting to be a part of their grandchildren's lives it's been a lonelier path than it should have been.

It's like we're all on the same wavelength when Jared picks Eleanor up from her bassinet and settles in next to me in the bed. "I know, Abi. We tried to—"

There's a soft knock at the door. No one is supposed to be due to check up on me or the babies for the next half-hour...and I made them both swear to me that they wouldn't start telling everyone until I'd had some downtime...

Lovely purple and white flowers are the first things I see around the curtain, followed by my eyes...my Dad's eyes. He and Nat shuffle into the room, the expressions of their faces somewhat unreadable until they take in the bundles in mine and Jared's arms.

Natalie's lip quivers just like mine, and I let out the biggest sob of all.

"Oh, Abi." Dad whispers, the first to take the steps closer to us. "They're beautiful." He sets the flowers. down on the table and leans down, his forehead up against mine. "I've been so stupid...I've been so damn stubborn." His tears mingle with mine, but I'm smiling because my dad is here, like I always imagined he would be.

Nat rushes to the boys, squeezing Jamie and pushing Jared's hair out of his face. When she leans in, she places a small kiss on Eleanor's cheek. "She smells heavenly," she laughs softly.

There's a flurry of commotion, both Dad and Nat anxiously kissing and loving on both of the girls, cooing at them even more than we have been. When I meet Jamie and Jared's gaze over their heads, I smile.

"We had to stop by and try to talk to them one last time," Jared says, his arm around Nat. "I couldn't stand the thought of them missing out anymore."

Natalie's smile turns down for a moment. "I'm so sorry, Abigail. We...we should've been here for you. All of you. But the boys came by and pretty much convinced us that it was time to let go of our issues and for us to be a proper family again."

"It doesn't even matter now. You're here. That's all I ever wanted," I whisper, leaning in to squeeze her.

There was a time when I imagined my life would turn out very differently. I thought I wanted to be with Cody. I thought I needed to turn my back on my stepbrothers and accept that my path had to take me in another direction.

I was prepared to turn my back on Jamie and Jared because I was scared. I didn't think that love would be enough but, as I gaze around at my perfect family, I can tell you that it is.

Love brought us together in the end.

And I'm forever glad that it did.

ABOUT THE AUTHOR

Stephanie Brother writes scintillating stories with bad boys and stepbrothers as their main romantic focus. She's always been curious about complicated relationships, and this is her way of exploring the situations that bring couples together and threaten to keep them apart. As she writes her way to her dream job, Ms. Brother hopes that her readers will enjoy the full emotional and romantic experience as much as she's enjoyed writing them.

Printed in Great Britain
by Amazon